He Had To Convince Her To Stay.

"I can give you twice your salary, plus stock options."

A triumphant grin spread across her face. "Done."

Only once he held her hand in his did he add, "Contingent, of course, on whether or not I find your father lessons satisfactory."

She frowned and tried to pull her hand away, but he held its delicate weight firmly in his own. "At the end of two weeks, I want Isabella to reach for me. Take it or leave it."

After a moment more of hesitation, she nodded. "It's a deal."

Only then did he release her hand.

He still felt the warmth of her palm against his and was struck by the impulse to fist his hand to contain the heat. Instead he wrapped the hand around Isabella.

"Don't worry, Isabella, she's not going to leave. I've just bought us two weeks to convince her to stay."

Dear Reader,

As I'm finishing up the line edits on this book, the prequel, *Baby on the Billionaire's Doorstep* is just now hitting shelves. I already have people asking after Derek, wondering when his book will be out.

In many ways, Raina and Derek's story doesn't begin with this book, but rather on page one of *Baby on the Billionaire's Doorstep*.

The moment Derek first saw Isabella, abandoned on his doorstep, he whipped out his cell phone and called his assistant, Raina…at one in the morning! I knew then that he would have to get his comeuppance and that Raina was just the woman to deliver it.

I've never before written two so closely linked stories. It was as challenging as it was rewarding. And I loved getting to revisit Isabella and watch her steal her way into another man's heart. I hope she, Derek and Raina find their way into your heart as well.

Enjoy!

Emily

BABY BENEFITS

EMILY McKAY

Published by Silhouette Books
America's Publisher of Contemporary Romance

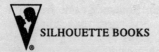

SILHOUETTE BOOKS

ISBN-13: 978-0-373-76902-5
ISBN-10:   0-373-76902-4

BABY BENEFITS

Visit Silhouette Books at www.eHarlequin.com

Printed in U.S.A.

Books by Emily McKay

Silhouette Desire

Surrogate and Wife #1710
Baby on the Billionaire's Doorstep #1866
Baby Benefits #1902

EMILY McKAY

has been reading romance novels since she was eleven years old. Her first Harlequin Romance came free in a box of Hefty garbage bags. She has been reading and loving romance novels ever since. She lives in Texas with her husband, her newborn daughter and too many pets. Her books have been finalists for RWA's Golden Heart Award, the Write Touch Readers' Award and the Gayle Wilson Award of Excellence. Her debut novel, *Baby Be Mine* was a RITA® Award finalist for Best First Book and Best Short Contemporary. To learn more visit her Web site at www.EmilyMcKay.com.

For my own copper-curled imp.

One

"What do you mean, she's mine?"

Derek Messina stared blankly at his brother, Dex. In his arms, Dex held a sleeping infant, which Derek pointedly did not look at.

The child could not be his.

True, sixteen days ago, she'd been left on his doorstep in the middle of the night with an ambiguous note pinned to her chest. Since his brother lived with him, it had been only logical to assume she was Dex's mess to sort out. Which was why—after they'd both taken a paternity test the next morning—Derek had left on a business trip to New York and Antwerp feeling confident the baby wasn't his.

"She can't be mine," he repeated firmly. But the

conviction in his voice couldn't block out the doubt and confusion that had begun to settle in his belly.

Dex merely looked at him with a wry smile. "She's yours."

Was that a hint of regret in Dex's voice?

"If this is your idea of a joke, it isn't funny."

"You think I would joke about this?" Dex shot him a look of annoyed disbelief. "No. Don't answer that. The results of the paternity test we both took are sitting over there on the counter."

With a growing sense of dread, Derek crossed to the kitchen counter where a short stack of papers sat. However, he couldn't quite force himself to pick them up. To face the possibility that his brother wasn't lying to him…

Because if he was honest with himself, he knew Dex wasn't. When they were just kids, Dex had pulled his share of pranks, but those days were long past.

No, if Dex said this baby was Derek's, then she was his.

Damn it.

The timing couldn't be worse. Not that there was a good time to find out you'd fathered a five-month-old.

Finally Derek picked up the papers and read them. Documentation that he was a genetic match for little Isabella Alwin. Just as Dex had claimed.

He looked up, gestured with the papers. "When did you find out?"

"Five days ago."

"And you didn't call me?"

Dex's gaze sharpened with something like distaste. "I didn't see any reason to. You wouldn't have cut your business trip short anyway."

True. But he definitely would have done things differently.

"I don't have to tell you how important this trip was," he said to Dex.

"Right, Messina Diamonds finally opened its diamond-cutting house in Antwerp. We're no longer just a family of uncouth miners. Now we're playing with the big boys." Bitterness laced Dex's words. "Of course that's much more important than your child."

The cynicism in Dex's voice snagged his attention, even through the fog of his shock. He studied his brother from across the room, noting the protective way Dex cradled the sleeping infant in his arms, the hand that cupped the back of her head, the way he shifted slowly from one foot to the other. If Derek didn't know better, he'd say Dex had been lulling babies to sleep all his life.

The peaceful tableaux roused his own cynicism. Dex was even less of a family man than he was. Two weeks of caring for a mewling infant couldn't have changed that. He'd bet good money on it. Except he wasn't a betting man.

Finally, Derek forced himself to look at the child. Downy copper-colored curls covered her head. Her cheek rested against Dex's chest. Impossibly long lashes lay against gently flushed cheeks. Her tiny rosebud of a mouth was parted. He might have thought she was a doll if it hadn't been for the moist half-moon of drool on Dex's shirt.

Turning his back on them both, he headed for the liquor cabinet in the living room. He poured two brandies and handed one to Dex, who had followed him. Somehow he looked almost natural holding a baby in one hand and a brandy in the other.

Resisting the urge to toss back his own drink, Derek took a careful sip before setting it aside. Shoving his hands deep into his pockets, he appraised her shrewdly. "She doesn't look like me."

Dex's gaze narrowed, as if annoyed. "She'd be a damn ugly baby girl if she did." After a moment of watching the child, he said, "She has Dad's eyes. Your eyes, too, I suppose."

His father's eyes? Well, wasn't that just a kick in the gut?

Though he supposed that was hardly her fault. Not that any of this was *her* fault. No, it was just bad timing and bad luck. And perhaps overconfidence on his part. He'd known there was a possibility she was his when he'd left on his trip for Antwerp, but he hadn't really believed it. That had been his mistake and his alone.

With a sigh of resignation, he said, "Then I suppose I should open a bottle of champagne or something. Welcome the other newest member of the Messina family."

Dex quirked an eyebrow. "The other newest member?"

"Yes," he said grimly. "I stopped by New York on my way to Antwerp and convinced Kitty to come on the trip with me."

"Kitty."

The censure in Dex's voice didn't surprise Derek. Dex had never liked Kitty, not that Derek had let that get in his way during the three years of calculated courtship it had taken to win her over.

"You aren't going to congratulate me?"

Dex raised the brandy snifter in a toast. "Congratulations. You got to spend two weeks with one of the most heartless women in the country."

He ignored Dex's dig. "Actually we had a very nice time."

"I hope you didn't plan to impress her with our office in Antwerp. She's probably been touring diamond cutting houses since she was a little girl."

"I should hope so." Kitty was an heir to the Biedermann Jewelry fortune. Her family owned the largest chain of jewelry stores in the country. "That's one of the reasons I've asked her to be my wife."

Dex choked on his brandy. "What. Don't tell me she said yes."

"Of course she did." Derek took no satisfaction in his brother's shocked expression. "I wouldn't have asked if I hadn't known she'd agree. Besides, she's a smart enough woman to see the business advantages to merging our families."

Dex looked down at the child sleeping in his arms. "What will she say when she finds out about Isabella?"

"I have no idea." Of course, that wasn't entirely true.

Kitty was beautiful and intelligent, with the business sense of a shark, all of which made her the perfect woman for him. She was not, however, the kind of woman to raise someone else's bastard child.

"This time, I'm definitely quitting." Raina Huffman gave herself a firm look in the mirror. She pressed her hands on the cool marble of the twentieth-floor executive women's bathroom. Despite the glare she gave herself, she wasn't quite convinced.

But it was time. Past time.

From behind her, a voice said, "You're not going to quit."

Raina spun around to see her friend Trinity standing with her hands on her hips and an amused expression on her pixielike face.

Raina narrowed her gaze. "I *am* going to quit."

"No, you're not. You never quit. You're always saying you're going to quit, but you never do."

As Trinity disappeared into one of the stalls, Raina frowned. "This time I mean it." She turned, propped her hip against the counter and began counting off items on her fingers. "I'm tired of being his errand girl. Of doing everything he wants the minute he wants it."

"You're his assistant, it's your job," Trinity countered smoothly.

"When he calls me at one in the morning on a Sunday and wants me to run a personal errand for him, that's not my job. It's a pain in the butt, that's what it is."

The toilet flushed and a second later Trinity emerged from the stall to wash her hands. "He may be a pain in the butt." She met Raina's gaze in the mirror. "He may even be the most demanding bastard of a boss in all of Dallas. Hell, he may make Meryl Streep in *The Devil Wears Prada* look like a fairy godmother. But you'll never quit because he pays you oodles and oodles of money. Which you need."

Raina had to stifle the urge to defend him. Plenty of people—Trinity included—joked about him being an evil dictator, however Raina knew better. Yes, he was a ruthless businessman and a demanding boss, but as his assistant and near constant companion, she saw sides of him that no one else did. However in addition to being generous and loyal, he was also intensely private and wouldn't appreciate her defending him to anyone.

So instead of thinking about his qualities that she would miss, she focused on something Trinity would understand.

"The oodles of money are nice." Raina sighed as she thought of all the money she'd made over the past nine years. Money she'd faithfully shuffled over to her mother's bank account to help raise her siblings. "But Kendrick is graduating in May. And Cassidy's scholarship came through again, so she's set for another two years. They're officially on their own."

"Which still leaves your mom to take care of."

"True, but the house is paid for." Thanks to those oodles and oodles of money. "And disability covers her living expenses." Raina smiled brightly. "So now I don't need the money anymore. I can walk away from this awful job and get a normal job. With normal hours. With a normal boss."

Trinity waggled her eyebrows. "With a boss who doesn't drive you crazy."

Right. Crazy. Or something.

She supposed "crazy" was as good a word as any. Derek frustrated her, angered her, made her want to tear out her hair. And occasionally tear off her clothes.

Truth was, she'd been his assistant for nine years,

eight of which she'd been slowly falling in love with him. It was a long time to pine for someone who saw her as "an indispensable cog" in his company, but not as a woman.

Her pitiful emotional state was something she didn't want to think about, let alone share with coworkers. She was afraid if she lingered much longer, she might give herself away. So she plunked her purse down on the counter and whipped out her tinted lip-gloss.

Beside her, Trinity just shook her head and chuckled. "You're not going to quit."

Holding the tube of lip-gloss in one hand, Raina said, "What?"

"You're putting on lip balm." Then she looked Raina up and down critically. "No, when you quit a creativity-smothering, life-sucking job like this after nine years, you don't wear practical shoes and lip balm. It calls for four-inch heels and bright red lipstick. It calls for a little ass-kicking."

Raina smiled wryly at her friend. "No, when *you* quit a job it may call for a little ass-kicking. As for me, I've never once walked into this building without looking like a professional. Today's no different. And again, I am definitely quitting."

"If you were quitting, you'd be willing to admit Derek's a heartless tyrant."

Raina forced a chuckle even as she said, "He's not so bad."

"Which is exactly what I knew you'd say. Which is why I maintain, you're not ready to quit."

"I sent my letter of resignation to the printer on my

way here," Raina protested. "Twenty minutes from now, I will no longer be an employee of Messina Diamonds. Well, twenty minutes and two weeks."

Trinity shrugged. "If you say so." And with that, she opened the door and headed out of the bathroom.

"Aren't you going to wish me luck?"

"I would if I thought you were really going to quit," Trinity said over her shoulder before disappearing down the hall.

Raina merely glared at her friend's retreating back.

Trinity was right. Oh, not about Raina's inability to quit, but about the job being creativity smothering and life sucking. In the nine years she'd been with Messina Diamonds, she'd worked more overtime than most people worked in a lifetime.

Whenever he needed something, Derek called her first. Whether it was two in the morning or a beautiful sunny Saturday. He wasn't an unreasonable man; he expected no more of her than he did of himself. He just expected a lot of himself.

She'd put up with the relentless hours for two reasons: the money couldn't be beat and she was infatuated with Derek. But it was time to cut the cord. Now that she didn't need the money anymore, she could quit, walk away and get on with her life. Stop entertaining these childish fantasies that one day he'd snap out of it, realize she was a woman and whisk her off for a romantic getaway to Aruba.

'Cause let's face it. If that was going to happen, it would have happened years ago.

Raina swung by the printer on the way to Derek's office. As she made her way through the halls, she scanned over the letter, reassuring herself that it was as succinct and professional as she remembered. No need to humiliate herself with any unnecessary displays of emotion.

She knocked once on the door to his office before entering. As always, his office smelled faintly of wood oil and the lingering citrus scent of Derek's cologne. He stood with his back to her, gazing out the bank of windows at the view of downtown Dallas his twentieth-floor window afforded him. The fine wool of his Italian tailored gray suit stretched across his back, accenting the breadth of his shoulders.

"Mr. Messina, may I have a word?"

"Thank God you're here, Raina." Derek turned around as he spoke. "We've got a lot to do today."

A pang of loss stabbed her chest at his words. He'd started nearly every day with those same words. Then her eyes dropped from his face to the sleeping baby he held in his arms.

Instantly any regret she felt was swept away by a wave of confusion.

"What are you doing with a baby?"

Derek's expression shifted and for an instant he looked as baffled as she felt.

"She's mine."

Raina's hand clenched involuntarily on the freshly printed letter of resignation, crumpling the crisp white paper. "Your baby? That's impossible."

"Normally I'd agree with you. But the results from the paternity test say otherwise." Derek's lips twisted into a grimace.

Someone who knew him less well might mistake the action for a wry smile, but Raina knew better. Derek never smiled. She felt as if the building had just been subjected to a mild earthquake. She could only imagine how he felt.

"Is that Isabella?"

"It is."

She stepped forward a few faltering steps, only to sink to the chair opposite Derek's desk.

"I don't understand. I thought she was Dex's child. The mother—Jewel or Lucy or whatever she was calling herself. She told me so herself."

"She lied." Almost as if she sensed she was the topic of conversation, Isabella began to squirm nervously in Derek's arm. He crossed to his chair and sat. "Jewel and Lucy are twins."

"So which one is Isabella's mother?"

"Jewel."

Raina sank back into her chair, trying to make sense of what little Derek was giving her. "So the woman I met last week, the woman Dex was so interested in, that was…"

"Lucy. Isabella's aunt. When Jewel abandoned Isabella on my doorstep, Lucy devised this crazy plan to get her niece back. She pretended to be her twin sister because she thought Dex would just let her take Isabella back."

"But Dex isn't really her father."

"No."

"And you are?"

"Apparently."

"So you and Dex slept with the same woman."

Derek's only response was a tight, uncomfortable nod. "That's weird."

"Not as weird as the fact that Dex has asked Lucy to marry him."

Raina cocked her head to the side and considered Derek. If he thought it was weird, then he must never have seen Lucy and Dex together. Raina had only seen them together once, but it had been obvious to her that they were well on their way to falling in love. At the time, it seemed only fitting, since they already had a child together. But if that child wasn't theirs, but was Jewel's and Derek's...

"So you slept with Jewel?" Distaste curdled her stomach. Jewel had been a Messina Diamond's employee over a year ago. She'd spent her entire, brief employment throwing herself at Derek. It had never occurred to Raina that Derek might have given in to the temptation Jewel presented.

For years, Raina had worked side by side with Derek and during that time, she'd fallen in love with his strength and loyalty. With his sheer determination to do the right thing by his family and company.

In all that time, he'd never given her any indication he saw her as a woman. Never glanced at her legs. Never let his touch linger on her hand. Never gazed into her eyes with the slightest hint of sexual curiosity.

She'd always told herself it was only because she was an employee. She'd comforted herself with the knowledge that he was honorable. That he would never, ever sleep with someone who worked for him.

To find out now that he'd slept with Jewel felt like

a crippling betrayal. Apparently, he wasn't too honorable to sleep with an employee. No, it was only Raina that he didn't want.

Two

Derek watched Raina from where he sat. She looked nearly as shocked as he felt.

This infant was his. This tiny sleeping child that he held awkwardly in his arms was the result of his stupidity. His mistake.

A sort of grim determination settled over him. He was going to make this work. And Raina would help him. They'd been through tougher things than this together.

"First off, I'm going to need you to clear off my schedule for the next two weeks."

Raina's head snapped up. "Clear off your schedule? Whatever for?"

Her frown of confusion didn't faze him. "I need to learn to be a father."

"Ignoring for a moment that you can't possibly learn to be a father in two weeks, there are several things on your schedule that can't possibly be moved."

"Anything that can't be moved either you or Dex will have to take care of. As for learning to be a father, Dex did it in two weeks. So can I."

"That's absurd. Dex didn't—"

"When I left for New York, Dex had no experience with children and even less interest in them. By the time I made it back, he'd bonded with her." He looked down at the child, searching for some semblance of a bond himself, but at the moment he felt only panic.

Raina shrugged. "The situation is hardly the same," she said weakly. "And yes, he certainly did seem smitten, back when he thought she was his daughter, but—"

"He's still—" Derek cast around for the right word, but couldn't find a better one than what she'd used. It seemed to curdle on his tongue. "Smitten. I had to argue with him to let me bring her to work with me today."

He couldn't say why it bothered him so—the way Dex seemed determined to protect Isabella from Derek's incompetence. He only knew that it did.

Raina merely frowned. "Why *did* you bring her to work with you? I thought Dex had hired a nanny?"

"He did. I've given her the next two weeks off."

"Why on earth—"

"Dex didn't have a nanny at first. That's probably why he bonded with her so quickly."

"Dex had Jewel—or rather Lucy—to help him."

"And I have you."

Her gaze narrowed and she jumped to her feet. The

crumpled ball of paper in her hand crackled as she squeezed it even tighter. "Oh, no, no, no. I am not taking care of this baby for you."

"I'm not—"

But she interrupted him, something she rarely did.

"You know, I've done a lot of crazy things for you over the years." She marched around his desk to glare at him. "I've worked weekends. I've missed vacations. I've given up holidays. I've gone on last-minute business trips where I've stayed in crappy hotels and eaten worse food. But this is where I draw the line."

Raina's tirade stunned him into momentary silence. If he didn't know better, he'd think she resented the work she'd done. But before he could ask, she spun away from him to pace the floor.

"I'm not helping you take care of that baby. I don't want anything to do with her. I don't care if she's yours." Her gaze flickered to Isabella and her expression softened for an instant before hardening again. "I don't care how cute she is."

He watched her with fascination. He'd never seen her like this. In all the years she'd worked for him— and it must be, what, eight or so by now—she'd always been the consummate professional. Well dressed, well-groomed, well-spoken. She'd never raised her voice. Never glared at him. Never showed so much as an ounce of disrespect.

Funny how he'd never realized before today how long her legs were, but now as she was striding across his room, they were hard to ignore. As was the way her cheeks flushed a pretty shade of pink when she raised her voice.

Something dangerously like desire stirred inside him as he watched her. He quickly stifled the reaction. This situation was strained enough as it was.

"Raina, I'd never ask you to do anything you're not comfortable with."

Her head whipped around toward him. "Not comfortable with?" She let loose a laugh that had a slightly maniacal tone to it. "You wouldn't ask that of me? How on earth would you even know what I'm comfortable with?"

This time, when he obviously had no response, she just stood there, waiting for him to answer. The moment stretched on seemingly forever and he felt his own inability to handle the situation spinning out of control.

Finally, she just shook her head. Then she stalked out of the room slamming the door behind her. He felt the concussive force of it like a physical thing.

To the empty room, he asked, "What the hell was that about?"

And where the hell had his calm, professional assistant disappeared to?

The only answer to his questions was the stirring of the tiny baby in his arms.

Woken by the slamming door, she twisted against his chest, pushing with all her five-month-old strength against the confines of his arms. When he didn't release her, she let out a wail of frustration.

He knew how she felt.

Raina didn't stop walking until she'd made it out to her car. She climbed in, slammed the door behind her, and pounded her fist on the steering wheel only to jump when she accidentally hit the horn. The blare of the horn echoed through the parking garage, causing several people to turn and gape in her direction.

Next she pounded her forehead against the steering wheel, an action that both released a tiny bit of her frustration and hid her face in case any of the people staring were her coworkers.

Or rather, ex-coworkers.

She glanced down at the paper still crumbled in her hand. Okay, soon-to-be ex-coworkers.

Why—in the middle of her ridiculous and embarrassing tirade—hadn't she at least had the sense to hand him her resignation? Or, in lieu of that, thrown it at him on the way out the door?

The timing had been perfect. She'd already made an ass out of herself. She might as well have removed the need to ever see him again. Besides, given her current state of rambling madness, he probably would have welcomed her resignation.

"So why didn't you just quit, you big dummy?"

She sighed, raised her forehead enough to rub at the tension there and then slouched deeper into her car seat.

"Probably because you're not really going to quit. At least not now."

How could she quit now? After all she'd done for him, all the late nights, all the weekends and holidays. How could she walk out on him when he needed her most? She alone knew how important family was to Derek. True, he had an odd way of showing it, but nothing mattered to him more. Which was probably why he was bungling things so badly right now.

Talk about big dummies.

He thought he could learn to be a father in two weeks? He thought he needed to, just because Dex had fallen hard for Isabella himself?

Men. Were they all this stupid or was it just the brilliant ones? Derek was a financial genius. He ran a multi-billion-dollar business. He was handsome, impeccably dressed and a whiz with the ladies. Yet when it came to some things, he was dumber than dirt.

And by "some things" she meant real relationships. Family. The things that mattered. And his daughter certainly fell into that category.

Raina straightened, considering the crumpled ball of paper in her hand. Maybe all wasn't lost after all. Maybe she could find a way to knock some sense into him over the next few weeks. As for her own emotional state…well, the thought of him sleeping with Jewel had certainly put a damper on her affections. And—if she were honest with herself—probably explained her outburst back in his office.

One thing was for certain. She wasn't going to sit in her car and cry, no matter how appealing doing so sounded.

As she climbed from the car, she muttered, "And damn that Trinity for being right. Does she have an actual, working Magic 8-ball or something?"

And if she did, what were the chances Raina could get her hands on it? Because she'd darn sure like to know how she was going to get through this without becoming even more emotionally involved than she already was.

"Sounds like you need some help in here."

Derek glanced up from the screaming infant to see

his brother standing in his office doorway. Just beyond Dex, in the reception area where Raina's now-empty desk sat, stood a cluster of curious onlookers, their heads tilted close together, their "concerned" whispers hung in the air as they angled for a view into his office. Apparently more than one person out there was eager to see him fail. Raina, had she been at her usual guard post, would have put a stop to the rubbernecking.

Damn Raina for leaving him when he needed her most. And damn Dex for wandering by to witness Isabella's rebellion.

"I don't need your help," Derek insisted, but Isabella ruined the effect by letting out a scream of protest so loud he thought it must have ruptured his eardrum.

Dex stepped into the office and closed the door behind him. "You sure about that?"

The bastard was smiling. As if this was just about the funniest thing he'd ever seen.

Isabella must have recognized Dex's voice, because she turned her head toward him. For an instant, her cries quieted. Then, no doubt sensing an ally, she redoubled her efforts to escape from Derek's arms. Derek felt each howl like a stab to the chest.

She pressed her tiny hands against his shoulder, shoving her upper body away from his. Since she obviously didn't want to be held against him, he hooked his hands under her armpits and held her at arm's length. Her protestations grew louder.

"Um, Derek, she doesn't like that."

Derek could only scowl. "You think?"

Before Dex could make any more smartass comments, Isabella kicked her legs out toward Derek. He instinctively sucked in his gut to stay out of range of her feet. As he did so, she squirmed again, nearly propelling herself out of his arms.

"Whoa, there." In a second, Dex crossed the room and pulled her from Derek's arms.

Instantly, Isabella quieted down. She curled up in the protection of Dex's arms and buried her face against his chest.

Resentment surged through Derek. Dex was his kid brother. Derek had spent his entire life protecting and taking care of him. And sure, sometimes he was a pain in the butt, but he was basically a good guy. So why did the sight of Isabella cuddled in his arms make Derek want to deck him?

Dex cradled her, slowly swaying back and forth. To Derek he said, "You need to be careful. You don't want to drop her."

Derek glanced at the stack of books on his desk. Drily, he said, "I bought fifteen books on child rearing at the bookstore this morning. I'm pretty sure one of them would have mentioned that it's better not to drop the baby on the floor."

Dex smiled. "Hey, I'm just trying to help. The learning curve here is pretty steep."

"It can't be too hard. You did it."

"I had help."

As he said the words, the door to the office swung open. Raina stood in the doorway, hands on her hips, a resentful scowl marring her delicate features.

"He'll have help, too. At least for a few weeks." She marched across the room to Dex. "Hand me that baby." Once she had Isabella in her arms, she pressed a hand to Dex's back. "Now, don't you have a job to be doing? Or at least a wedding to plan or something?"

"I was just helping," Dex protested.

"No. You thought you were helping. What you were actually doing was butting in. You learned to do this without Derek breathing down your neck, he should get to do the same thing. As it is now, you're just making him nervous."

Dex grinned.

"He isn't—" Derek started.

"Yes, he is. Besides, if you're going to try to learn to be a father in two weeks—" Sarcasm dripped from her voice, making it clear she thought he was insane "—then the last thing you need to be thinking about is how this genius does things. Trust me when I tell you, he's no expert."

"Hey—" Dex protested.

She turned her glare back in his direction. "I mean it. For the next two weeks, I don't want to see you anywhere near here. You're always complaining about not having enough responsibility at work, well, here's your chance. Go find something to do. Goodness knows, Derek is going to be too busy to work for the next two weeks. And while you're at it, I hope you're planning on spending a lot of time with Lucy, because Derek doesn't need you hanging around the house, either."

Dex grinned as he allowed himself to be shuffled toward the door. To Raina he said, "I guess you decided to finally push back." Before leaving he looked up at Derek one last time. "One word of advice—babies eat every two hours."

Every two hours? "That can't be right."

"It is. I swear. Oh, and babies don't eat pizza."

Raina glared. "Of course they don't eat pizza."

"I'm just saying…" He didn't finish the sentence, but retreated through the door, hands held up in the universal sign of surrender.

Derek made a mental note for himself. No pizza.

When the door closed behind Dex, Derek turned his attention to Raina. She held Isabella cradled in her arms, murmuring soothing nonsense to the baby. As Isabella settled into her arms, tension seemed to drain away from Raina. She tucked her face to the top of Isabella's head and inhaled deeply.

For an instant, an expression crossed her face unlike any he'd ever seen before. The mixture of serenity and yearning nearly took his breath away. Raina, who he'd always thought of as merely pretty, was beautiful.

The moment passed so quickly he might have imagined it. Then she was looking up at him again as fierce annoyance flickered across her face. Once again, an expression he'd never before seen. But this time decidedly less pleasant, and perhaps easier to deal with.

"Here's the deal," she began. "Let me make it clear that I think you're being ridiculous. It shouldn't matter that Isabella has a close bond with her uncle. You should be glad she has people who care about her in her life. Having said that, if you really think you have to compete with Dex and learn to be a father in two weeks, then I'll spend that time teaching you everything I know about children."

"Which I suppose is considerable." He didn't bother to keep the note of sarcasm out of his voice. He had no doubt Raina could master anything she set her mind to.

She could certainly help him learn, but how much did she already know?

Almost as if she was reading his mind, she countered with, "I have four younger brothers and sisters. I've been around babies all my life."

"Four? I had no idea you had that many brothers and sisters."

"Yes, four. And of course you didn't. It would never occur to you to ask. You just don't pay that close attention."

He frowned, fairly certain she'd just insulted him. Something else she'd never done before today. "What's gotten into you?"

Her gaze narrowed. "You want to know what's gotten into me?" With her free hand, she pulled out the crumpled sheet of paper he'd noticed earlier and tossed it at him. "This. This is what's gotten into me."

The paper bounced off his chest and fell to the floor. He didn't bother to pick it up. Raina had worked for him for a long time. He knew her as well as he knew anyone. Whatever had brought about this sudden change in her attitude, he'd find a way to fix it.

"Whatever is on that sheet of paper, whatever has you so upset, we'll work it out."

"Not this time. That's my letter of resignation."

Raina watched Derek's expression shift from his normal confidence to confusion and shock with more than a modicum of regret. This was so not how she'd imagined this conversation going.

She'd envisioned herself sitting across from his desk, carefully outlining her reasons for leaving, him frowning with regret, but eventually standing up, shaking her hand, and watching her walk out. In her mind, it had all been very dignified.

She had not imagined throwing things at him.

Nor had she imagined holding in her arms this sweet baby girl.

Even as the thought went through her mind, she squashed it as ruthlessly as she had her doubts about quitting. This child in her arms was not a "sweet baby girl." She was a booby trap. She was a cuddly little bundle of emotional attachment.

If Raina thought it was going to be hard to walk away from Derek, this little cutie pie would only make it that much harder.

Which was why, as soon as Isabella began to quiet down, Raina scanned the room for somewhere to place her. When she didn't see one, she crossed to where Derek stood.

"Okay, lesson one. Babies like to be held close to your body. Let her hear your heartbeat. Let her feel you breathing slowly in and out. Here, try it." She placed the baby into his arms and then quickly distanced herself from them both.

For an instant, they wore identical expressions of confusion and surprise. Isabella immediately started squirming again. This time, he brought her close to his chest and it seemed to calm her.

"And just remember, babies are like a savvy business rival. They can sense your insecurities. When you're nervous, don't let her know it."

As Derek glanced down at the infant in his arms, determination narrowed his gaze. She watched him following her advice, deliberately slowing his breathing with the steady rise and fall of his chest. Then he looked back at her. "You're resigning?"

"That was the plan."

"You can't resign."

Had he and Trinity been comparing notes or something? "Trust me, I can resign."

"You've worked here for eight years. Why would you want to resign now?"

The blank confusion nearly did her in. He honestly couldn't imagine her wanting to do anything else. It was charming in a way, his absolute conviction that she was as devoted to the company as he was. His total faith in her.

"Nine," she admitted with a sigh. "I've worked here for nine years. It's time for me to move on."

"You have another job? A better offer? I'll match it."

His confidence sent a jolt of panic through her. Negotiations were second nature to him. If she wasn't careful, he'd bargain her into submission before she knew what was happening.

If he knew the real reason she'd come back... If he knew that she'd simply been unable to walk out on him when he needed her...well, if he knew that, she'd be doomed.

No, she needed something to throw him off the scent. Luckily, she'd been watching him closely all these years. She'd learned a thing or two from him.

"I don't have another offer. I'm not leaving because of money or benefits packages. I'm leaving because I just don't want to work here anymore."

"I don't believe you. You love this job. You love this company."

His voice was filled with fierce passion. She could only shake her head.

"No, *you* love this job. *You* love this company. Me? I just work here." She shrugged, hoping the indifferent gesture would counteract the wistfulness of her tone. "For me, it's always been about the money. You've paid better than anyone else in town. And if you want the truth, it's still about the money."

A less desperate woman might have balked at taking advantage of his situation. But Raina remembered all the times she'd watched him browbeat a business rival. Determined not to be a causality of his superior skills, she pushed ahead, refusing to candy coat the situation.

"The way I see it, after I hand in my resignation, I can take the two weeks of vacation I have socked away. Or I can stick around and help you with this little problem of yours." She gestured toward Isabella. "So you should ask yourself—if I'm not here to help, what exactly are you going to do with this daughter of yours?"

His gaze narrowed just a bit. He was sizing her up, measuring her weaknesses. She didn't let any of them show.

"What's your price?"

"I don't want to quit. I want you to fire me."

Three

Derek had always told people that Raina was smarter than most of the board members. This proved he was right. Unfortunately.

"If I fire you, you'll qualify for unemployment."

"And a compensation package."

She stood maybe eighteen inches away from him, her gaze squarely on his, her chin bumped up, her spine stiff enough to give her the illusion of another inch or so of height he knew she didn't really possess. Her arms crossed over her chest in a way that plumped up her breasts.

She couldn't possibly know how alluring she appeared at this moment. Plenty of women used their physical assets as business assets. Raina wasn't one of them.

Still, just because she didn't know the edge her body

gave her, that didn't mean he was unaffected by it. Quite the contrary, in fact.

A situation was made worse by the infant he held in his arms. Raina's assurances that Isabella was nothing more than a business rival had done little to boost his confidence. Isabella squirmed fitfully in his arms. Clearly she knew he was an amateur and didn't want anything to do with him.

Confronted with Raina's newfound aplomb on one front and Isabella's mutiny on the other, he felt besieged in a way he hadn't since taking over as CEO of Messina Diamonds.

"What kind of severance package are you talking about?"

For the first time in the conversation, Raina hesitated. Aha. So she hadn't thought this far ahead.

But she quickly recovered and said in a rush, "I want what Schmidt got when she left."

He nearly chuckled at her ballsy display. "Schmidt was a VP. And she'd been with Messina for over ten years."

"Only nine and half, if you subtract the six months of unpaid leave she took to tour the wine country for her honeymoon. Besides, you've told me more than once that I was more valuable than any VP." She arched an eyebrow coolly, looking for the first time today like her normal self. "Do you need me to scour your old e-mails to find that statement in writing?"

"That won't be necessary."

Isabella shot him a dirty look as she wedged a tiny fist under his chin and pushed with inhuman strength. Since he was clearly losing control of the Isabella portion of the equation, he needed to wrap things up with Raina quickly. It wouldn't help his position for her to see how desperate his situation was. "I can't give you the same package as Schmidt, the board will never stand for it. But I can give you twice your salary, plus stock options."

A triumphant grin spread across her face. "Done."

She extended her hand to him. Only once he held it in his, did he add, "Contingent, of course, on whether or not I find your father lessons satisfactory."

She frowned and tried to pull her hand away, but he held its delicate weight firmly in his own.

"Define satisfactory. In specific terms. I don't want to get to the end of the two weeks and have you back out of our deal on a technicality."

"Would I do that?"

"In a minute. 'Satisfactory' is entirely too vague."

"Then how about this." He thought briefly of the piercing pain he'd felt watching his daughter sobbing as she reached for Dex. "At the end of two weeks, I want Isabella to reach for me."

Raina narrowed her gaze. "That's not—"

"When Dex is in the room." Her frown deepened and he could see her looking for an out. A bargain more easily met. "Take it or leave it."

After a moment more of hesitation, she nodded. "It's a deal."

Only then did he release her hand. As he slid his hand from hers, he was struck by the delicacy of her bone structure. Such a contrast to the strength of her handshake, as if all the force of her will had been concentrated down into that one simple movement.

She turned and all but pranced from the room, her step lightened in a way he'd never before seen. As if she were overjoyed to be leaving him.

He, on the other hand, still felt the warmth of her palm against his and was struck by the impulse to fist his hand to contain that heat, as if he could hold on to a little bit of her that much longer. Instead he wrapped the hand around Isabella's chest, held her out to look her over.

He waited for some pang of paternal recognition. Maybe the groundwork for fatherly bonding. Instead, he felt only discomfort. Inadequacy. Incompetence. So he did what he always did when faced with an obstacle. He bluffed.

"Don't worry, Isabella," he began, only to hesitate over her name. Isabella sounded so formal for such a squirmy little bundle.

Studying her face, he ran down a list of nicknames. Bella? No, too…girly. Izzie? Out of the question. That's what Dex called her. Well, crap.

"Don't worry, kid. She's not really going to leave. I've just bought us two weeks to convince her to stay."

And he had to convince her to stay. He relied on her too much to let her go. There was no way he'd make it through this without Raina's help.

And he had a lot in his favor. For starters, he'd seen her expression when she'd held Isabella. The kid was a charmer for sure. She'd win Raina back, even if he couldn't.

Which meant he had a plan for dealing with only one of the women in his life. As for Kitty, that was another matter entirely. He'd been avoiding her calls ever since he'd returned home to find out the news about Isabella.

He knew postponing the conversation wouldn't make it any easier. But so far, he had no idea how to break the news to her. He'd been in crisis mode, dealing with Isabella for the past day and a half. A cardinal rule of business was that you first put out the fire most likely to burn down your house.

Of course, now that he had a plan for dealing with Isabella and had convinced Raina to stay on for now, it was time to tell Kitty she was about to become a stepmother.

Almost as if she knew she'd been relegated to the back burner, Isabella scrunched her face up and let out a howl of protest. Unsure of what else to do, Derek sank into his executive leather chair. Holding the screaming child on his lap, he rocked slowly back and forth as exhaustion ate away at his patience.

How could one little infant cause this many problems?

Sometimes, she wondered if she had any brains at all.

"So you didn't quit?" Raina's sister Lavender asked from her spot at the kitchen counter where she was tossing a salad.

Raina, sitting at the table, stacked her fists on the tabletop and propped her chin on top of them. Tonight, the scent of French bread warming in the oven and spaghetti sauce simmering on the stovetop wasn't as comforting as it should have been. "No, I didn't quit. Not exactly."

"I knew you wouldn't," quipped Kendrick as he strolled through the doorway, nonchalantly dropping his backpack onto the chair beside Raina.

Lavender glared at him as she brushed a strand of light brown hair off her forehead. "Be supportive."

Kendrick shrugged, swiping a bite of tomato off Lavender's cutting board as he continued on his way to the living room to where their mother sat, watching her nightly dose of CNN. "Hey, I call 'em like I see 'em."

Raina lifted her head up just long enough to call, "And don't leave your backpack in the kitchen."

Without looking back, he waved a hand as if to say he'd get it later. It didn't make her feel any better.

"Of course I didn't really quit. Apparently I have no spine. Even my brother ignores me."

Lavender chuckled as she scraped the tomatoes into the bowl. "Of course he ignores you. He's seventeen. He ignores everyone." Lavender cocked her head to one side, her hazel eyes suddenly serious as she studied Raina. "So?" she prodded gently. "What happened? Why didn't you quit? Did Darth Vader bully you?"

"Oh, what's the point in rehashing it all?" Raina stood, ignoring Lavender's slur against Derek. Cassidy, the youngest of Raina's three sisters, had nicknamed Derek "Darth Vader" years ago. Because—in Cassidy's words—he was "tall, dark, and intimidating. And pure evil." Unfortunately it had stuck.

While it had been amusing at first, her family's intense dislike of Derek only made her feel awkward now. If her siblings only knew how much he'd done for their family... Well, they'd be embarrassed to say the least. However, if they knew how she really felt about Derek, then they'd just be baffled.

Sidetracking the question, Raina asked, "Don't you need help with dinner?"

But Lavender held up a hand in protest. "No way. Tomorrow night is your night to do dinner. And I happen to know that Kendrick let you help with last night's tacos. Besides, I suspect you're just trying to distract me." She pointed the chef's knife at Raina with a mock scowl. "Now 'fess up."

"It's not that I didn't quit, it's just that it didn't go exactly as I'd planned." She struggled to put her feelings into words. When she'd stormed out of his office, she'd felt confident. Sure she'd made the right decision. Won a major victory. But the more she thought about it, the more she wondered if she'd been outsmarted.

Lavender made a "keep it coming" gesture, so Raina summed up the agreement she'd made with Derek. As Raina spoke, Lavender's chopping slowed, then stopped all together as she focused her attention on Raina's story.

"So after two weeks, he's supposed to fire you?"

"Yep."

"Well." Lavender cocked her head to the side. "That sounds like a good thing. All you have to do is make it through the next two weeks, win this bet you've got going with him and walk away with a bundle of money."

"That's if I can get Isabella to respond to him," Raina pointed out, her sense of dread building.

"True. But that shouldn't be so hard to do."

"Easy for you to say. You're the early childhood development major. Me, I passed myself off as some kind of expert on kids."

"You helped Momma raise four kids. I'd say you are an expert."

"Did you miss the part where I said Isabella is five months old? Sure, if she was fifteen or even five, maybe I'd be a help. But Momma didn't get sick until I was nineteen. Before that I was just an ordinary kid with younger brothers and sisters. There's certainly nothing in my background that makes me an expert on infants."

"Don't sell yourself short. You're great with babies. They love you. And you certainly adore—" Lavender broke off, frowning. "Oh. That's what you're worried about."

"What?" Raina tried to keep her expression blank, but failed miserably.

"You're worried you're going to fall in love with this kid of his. That after a couple of weeks of dealing with the charming little tot, you won't want to quit. You'll be afraid of leaving her at the mercies of Darth Vader."

"I—" She started to deny it, but then shrugged. Why bother? "I guess I am."

Yes, the girl was adorable. And yes, Raina nursed a serious hankering to scoop the imp up in her arms, nuzzle her head, and suck in a big ol' lungful of baby smell. And of course, the idea of getting attached to Isabella scared her. After all, she'd made a pledge to herself. Kids were not in her immediate future. It was time to put her own needs first for once.

But Isabella was only part of the problem. It was

Derek who really had her worried. He was hard enough to resist as it was. Toss in an adorable kiddo and Raina may well be doomed. After all, was there anything sexier than a man with a baby? Look what had happened to Lucy, after all. She'd fallen for the Dex/Isabella combo like a ton of baby formula. Raina, already nine-tenths of the way to hopelessly devoted to Derek, didn't stand a chance.

Of course, she couldn't explain *that* to Lavender. She just wouldn't get it. Raina had exerted far too much effort over the years convincing her family Derek was a jerk. They saw him as…well, the nickname said it all.

Lavender would never understand how Raina had seen past all that to fall in love with him.

She dropped her head back into her hands. "I should have just quit. If I'd stuck to my original plan, I'd never have to even walk into the office again."

Let alone see Derek, she added to herself with misery.

"So do it."

"What?" Raina looked up.

"Go back there tomorrow and quit. For real this time." Lavender sliced through a carrot with a blood-thirsty flourish. "Go all Donald Trump on him and fire *his* sorry butt." She punctuated each of the last four words with an emphatic chop.

Raina tried not to wince. "But the money," she protested.

"Forget the money."

"I can't forget the money. That bonus is the difference between whether I leave Messina Diamonds to look for another job as an executive assistant or go back to culinary school."

Lavender rolled her eyes, then opened her mouth and snapped it shut again several times in an exaggerated mime of struggling for words.

"What?" Raina asked innocently.

"Don't you 'what' me." Lavender pointed the tip of the knife in Raina's direction. "How many times do we have to go over this? You are not allowed to go back to work. You've served your time. The next stop for you is culinary school."

"Which costs a load of money. Which I don't have. Which means, the next stop for me is gainful employment."

"You have money, you just don't want to spend it."

Raina pressed her lips together. "How do you know—"

"Momma told me, of course. Did you really think she'd keep secret a savings account with that much money in it?"

"That money isn't mine," Raina stated firmly.

"Of course it's yours. You earned it."

"I earned it for Momma. And you kids."

"You've been providing for Momma and us for nearly a decade now." Lavender's tone made it sound like a bad thing. "It's time to provide for yourself for a change. Besides, we are doing fine. You said so yourself. Momma's got disability checks, the house is paid for, and we all have scholarships and financial aid."

Lavender looked so smug, Raina didn't bother to argue with her. Raina wouldn't be dipping into the family's savings to pay her tuition to culinary school. Yes, for the moment, everyone was provided for. But Raina knew all too well that accidents could happen without warning. Her mother's stroke nine years ago had taught her that lesson.

But there was no point in arguing with Lavender about it. And thankfully, Raina was saved from having to do so by the ringing of her cell phone. Not her personal cell phone, but her always-on, always-had-to-answer-it work cell phone.

She'd developed a strict rule about not talking to Derek during dinner with her family, but otherwise, she was accessible twenty-four hours a day. Since they hadn't yet sat down at the table, she pulled the phone from her pocket, glancing at the number as she did so. She didn't recognize it, but was relieved to see the New York area code. The last thing she needed was to talk to Derek right now.

"Raina here."

"Louraina Huffman?" asked a disdainful woman's voice.

"Yes."

"The Louraina Huffman who's Derek Messina's assistant?" The voice seemed to imply that maybe some other Raina Huffman had swiped the phone for nefarious purposes.

"Yes," Raina repeated.

"Well, then, I'll need you to get a hold of him. I've been calling for the past day and a half and haven't reached him. It's been most inconvenient."

Raina nearly chuckled, despite her grim mood. Whoever this lady was, she was clearly put out.

Somehow it just lightened her spirits knowing that some pretentious woman in New York was having a hard time with Derek, too.

Keeping her humor to herself, she said in her most professional voice, "If you'll just leave me your name and number I'll pass them on to him immediately."

"This is Kitty."

She couldn't place the name, so she asked, "And you are?"

"His fiancée."

He'd known very few people in his life whose strength of will matched his own. Isabella, apparently, was one of those rare individuals.

Not that fortitude, perseverance and pure mule-headedness were bad qualities in a daughter. He just wished she hadn't aimed them all at him. Or that she'd do so more quietly.

By nine-thirty, after less than six hours alone with Isabella, he'd given in and called Mrs. Hill to take over. The only thing worse than Mrs. Hill's cloying sympathy when she showed up at his house was the smug expression on Isabella's face. If he didn't know better, he'd swear she was gloating.

This minor setback only fueled his determination. She was his daughter. He would make her love him.

However, despite his resolution to win her over, Isabella still seemed set against him. And apparently she'd convinced Mrs. Hill, as well.

This morning, when he'd told the nanny she could go home, Mrs. Hill had practically smirked her disbelief. She'd left him three different numbers he could reach her at and offered more than once to check back in come nightfall. As he'd watched her leave, grim resolve had settled in his belly. Last night, he'd given in to his own insecurities and called for backup, but tonight would be different. After all, he had Raina coming to the house to work her magic.

Isabella, well fed after being given a bottle by Mrs. Hill, was bouncing happily in some kind of spring-loaded seat on the living-room floor. For the moment, she appeared satisfied to play with the toys ringing the seat, but he knew from yesterday afternoon's experience that things could go from peaceful to piercingly loud with little warning.

He was just glancing at his watch when the doorbell rang. Even though Raina had a key to the house for emergencies, she always rang the bell. He found her on the other side of the door with her arms crossed over her chest, her foot tapping like mad.

"You have a fiancée?" were the first words out of her mouth.

"What?" he asked before her question even sank in.

"A fiancée," she repeated slowly, as if he were mentally impaired. "As in a woman whom you are planning to marry."

"Oh, Kitty." Truth be told, he hadn't given Kitty much thought over the past two days. He hadn't exactly forgotten about her, but his intention to call her had fallen by the wayside when faced with Isabella's tantrums. Telling Kitty he had a daughter would be hard enough. Explaining why that daughter seemed to hate him was more than he was up for at the moment.

"Yes. Kitty." Raina pronounced each word succinctly, like she were spitting out watermelon seeds that had been dipped in battery acid. "You failed to mention that you'd gotten engaged. Did it just slip your mind?"

Once again, his cool, professional Raina had been replaced by someone hotheaded and out-spoken. Not to mention someone dressed a tad less professionally than normal.

He looked pointedly at Isabella. "I've been a bit preoccupied."

"Obviously, or your fiancée wouldn't have to call me at home three times last night."

"She called you three times and you're just now giving me the messages?"

"Well," she propped her hands on her denim-clad hips, "that's what you get for not answering the phone."

"I had to turn the phone off. Isabella cried every time it rang."

The annoyed look she shot him should have countered at least some of her appeal. It didn't.

He studied her, hoping to discern why he suddenly found her so fascinating. Instead of her usual dark business slacks or calf-length skirts, she wore simple blue jeans. Instead of a jacket and button up white blouse, she wore a copper-colored T-shirt. The effect should have been quite ordinary. After all, he'd seen a multitude of women dressed in jeans and T-shirts. Such casual clothes looked good on some, made others look dowdy or work worn. They rarely made anyone look like a sex goddess.

Yet on Raina, that was somehow the effect. The jeans were slim-fitting, drawing his attention to the hitherto unknown fact that her legs stretched on forever. The T-shirt was soft and worn, falling just below her waistband, tempting him with the possibility it might reveal a swath of her midriff. Suddenly he was aware that, instead of the multiple layers of bulky shirt and jacket that usually barricaded her breasts from his gaze, today there was only a single layer of cotton. And probably one of silk.

He had to force his eyes back to her face, only to find her glaring at him. "What's wrong with you this morning?"

Swallowing past the lump in his throat, he said, "You don't normally dress so…informally."

"Of course not." She stepped forward into the entry-way.

A better man would have backed away, given her the space to pass without brushing against him. However he couldn't resist that seemingly innocent contact. Her gaze darted to his as their shoulders brushed. That in-stant of eye contact was the only indication that she, too, felt the heat between them. Her voice, when she spoke, was as brisk and unaffected as normal.

"This isn't exactly a normal work situation," she continued, striding past him into the living room. "If we're not going into the office, then I'm not wearing a suit."

He followed her into the living room and was faced with the first major flaw of his plan to have Raina teach him parenting skills. Raina stood in the middle of the living room, hands propped on hips, accentuat-ing their narrow width and the gentle curve of her bottom. Her hair tumbled over her shoulder as she cocked her head to one side, studying the chair where Isabella sat.

The image she presented was temptingly informal. And somehow right at home. In his home.

Naturally, she'd been to his house many times before. But never before had he been struck by how natural it seemed to have her there.

She looked over her shoulder to where he stood, struck dumb—apparently—in the doorway. "Well, you had her alone overnight and you didn't kill her. That's a start."

"I had to call the nanny."

"Figures," she muttered with a derisive snort. "Well, no one would expect to be able to handle an infant all alone on the first night. That's just crazy."

The insult was obvious. She thought he was crazy. Raina, who'd never so much as criticized his penmanship without the utmost tact, had just insulted him.

He gave her a thoughtful look. "You're mad at me," he observed.

"Why would I be mad?" she asked, her tone icy.

"Something about Kitty, I'm guessing."

"Hmm." But she ignored his comment and squatted down beside Isabella. "When was the last time you fed her?"

"Mrs. Hill fed her just before she left." He crossed to stand beside her, noticing the way Isabella sized her up. "Around seven."

"Ah, so you haven't fed her yourself yet, have you?"

"No. And you're avoiding the question."

Raina stood and suddenly she was unexpectedly close. "It wasn't a question. You guessed that I was angry. And you guessed that it was because of Kitty. Neither of those was a question."

He caught a whiff of her scent. Something he'd never noticed before, something warm and homey.

Gazing up at him, her eyes seemed huge. How had he never before noticed what a warm shade of brown her eyes were? Like his finest Scotch.

She, too, must have been surprised to find herself so close to him, because she sucked in a deep breath and stepped back nervously.

He followed her step for step, not giving her room to retreat. "Well? Am I right? Are you upset about Kitty?"

She licked her lips and in that same chilly tone, asked, "Why would I be upset about Kitty?"

"I don't know. You tell me."

"You certainly have the right to get engaged to any virtual stranger at a moment's notice. Without any fore-thought or planning."

"Kitty Biedermann isn't a stranger. I've known her for years."

"Well, then, there you have it. She's an old family friend. Of course you'd marry her. For all I know, you've been silently carrying a torch for her for years. Decades maybe. It's none of my business."

"It's not like that."

"It doesn't matter, does it? I'm just your assistant. You've never confided that kind of personal information in me anyway." She frowned. "And I'm not even your assistant anymore. At least, I won't be two weeks from now."

Four

Raina knew she was giving herself away. Just like she knew Derek would pounce on any sign of weakness. Getting overly emotional about this would do no good. He'd only use it against her. She'd certainly seen him do that to many a business rival.

With forced calm, she marched over to the ExerSaucer where Isabella sat and crouched down. But after a second, she ignored her own advice, stood again, and spun back toward him as the name of this new fiancée finally sunk in.

"Wait a second…Kitty Biedermann? As in Biedermann Jewelry?"

He didn't even have the sense to look embarrassed. "Yes, Kitty is the daughter of Randal Biedermann."

Something akin to disgust washed over her. Somehow, it bubbled out of her as a slightly demented giggle. "There's a Biedermann's Jewelry in every mall in America."

"Actually, Biedermann's are in fewer than eighty percent of malls."

"Still, you're marrying into the biggest jewelry chain in the country."

How could she possibly compete with that?

Not that she was trying to. Of course she wasn't. She had no chance of winning his heart regardless of whether he was engaged to Kitty Biedermann or Scooby-Doo.

She *knew* that. And yet the thought made her heart constrict in her chest. Not only for herself—though the thought of him marrying another woman was almost too much to bear—but also for him.

Raina may never have met Kitty Biedermann, but she certainly knew the Biedermann family reputation of wealth, privilege and social standing. A woman with that kind of background could never understand Derek. She couldn't begin to make him happy.

But happiness hadn't played into Derek's bride selection. This was nothing more than a business decision and even still Raina knew she could never compete.

"You think it's a bad idea."

She cut her gaze to him, instantly suspicious. "I couldn't care one way or another," she lied.

"Kitty is the perfect woman for me."

Suppressing a sigh of frustration, she forced a nod. "I'm sure she is. She's rich and in the jewelry business. What's not to love?"

"I thought you said it didn't bother you?" His lips twitched without parting into a true smile.

What was worse? Knowing that he was making a huge mistake and not being able to do anything to stop him or having him be amused by her reaction?

"Okay." She spun around to face him, nine years of pent-up advice bubbling to the surface. "You want to know the truth?"

The hint of his smile vanished. "I've always valued your opinion. Though in the past you've been less brutally honest."

"Don't forget you asked for this." She sucked in a deep breath. It must be true that old habits die hard, because she practically had to force herself to actually voice her opinion. It felt good being as honest with him about a personal matter as she had always been about business. "I do think this is a huge mistake. You hardly know this woman."

"Actually, I really have known her for years."

"But certainly not well. I manage your business and social schedule. You've never even mentioned her before now."

"I've been courting Kitty for a while. You don't know everything about my schedule, Raina." His tone was somehow both gentle and chiding. "You can't believe you've known about every woman I've dated since hiring you."

She felt his words like a punch in the gut. And here he'd accused her of brutal honesty.

"Of course not," she scoffed to save face, because somehow she'd believed exactly that. She'd scheduled his biannual teeth cleaning and his monthly haircuts when his hair began to curl over his ears. She'd made the reservations when he took business associates to

dinner and his appointments with his CPA. She'd
scheduled his visits to get his blood pressure checked,
for goodness sake.

She wasn't just his professional assistant, but his
personal one, as well. She'd canceled dates and on
occasion planned them. She'd returned phone calls and
ordered flowers. In all that time, there hadn't been a lot
of women, but there'd been enough that she'd assumed
she knew about all of them.

Until she'd found out about Jewel. And as if she
hadn't felt that betrayal deeply enough, now there was
this other woman she hadn't known about at all. Not
just a woman, but the woman he wanted to marry.

Had she known him at all? Was it really him she
loved or just some fantasy man she'd idealized in her
mind?

"Well," she said with a prosaic shrug and a pointed
look at Isabella. "Obviously I didn't know about all the
women you've dated."

"About Jewel—" he began, but she cut him off.

"No. You don't need to explain." And she *really*
didn't want to hear any of the details about that. "I can
do the math. I figure you had the affair with her about
the time your father died."

Figuring that out had somehow made her feel better.
Okay, so he'd slipped up. In his grief he'd done something he'd normally never do. It could happen to
anyone.

But instead of giving her the reassurances she se-
cretly wanted to hear, he said, "I was going to say that
my lawyer's drawing up the custody papers and I'll
need you to go get them later this week."

"Custody papers?" Betrayal sliced through her gut. Even now, even in the midst of this intimate conversation, he treated her like an errand boy.

"Yes, Lucy's been talking to Jewel. She convinced her to grant me full custody of Isabella, with visitation rights for Jewel, though I doubt she'll exercise them." His lips pressed into a grim line. "She'll be too busy spending all the money I'm paying her for the privilege of raising her child."

She might have felt sorry for him if she hadn't still been smarting from the twist their conversation had taken. Here she'd been thinking he was about to finally open up, to share his feelings with her. Instead, he was just using her as a courier.

Why, for goodness sake, had she ever allowed herself to get so emotionally involved with a man who saw her as little more than a fancy PDA?

If she'd said it once, she'd said it a thousand times. Enough was enough.

This was proof it was time to put her hands in the air and step slowly away from the job.

"Well, then," she said grimly. "If this Kitty Biedermann is such a catch, I can't see why you need me. She should be the one here helping you with Isabella."

A long pregnant silence stretched between them while she waited for him to respond.

"You haven't told her yet, have you?" she finally asked as a sense of dull resignation settled over her.

This time, at least, he had the good sense to look sheepish. Or as close to sheepish as a man as arrogant as he was could look. His lack of response was answer enough.

"I should have known."

"I will tell her," he stated with enough conviction she had to wonder exactly who he was trying to convince.

"Oh, I'm sure you will. Otherwise she'll wonder who the kid growing up in her house is."

Derek stared blankly at her. That's what she got for trying sarcasm on someone who took everything so seriously.

Despite her frustration with him at the moment, years of working with him, of being his first line of defense took over and she found herself saying, "You have to tell her. Soon. When I spoke with her yesterday evening, she said you hadn't been answering your cell phone. Which means you're dodging her calls."

"I'm not dodging her calls. I'm waiting for the opportune moment to tell her the truth."

Raina fisted her hands. "She's your fiancée. The woman you're presumably planning on spending the rest of your life with. The opportune moment to tell her you have a child would have been about five seconds after you found out."

Raina looked as if she were barely controlling the urge to hit him with something and the expression on her face screamed, *You're an idiot!*

Yeah, tell me something I don't know, he considered saying. And he certainly wasn't used to needing anyone else's help to sort out his problems.

Perhaps he should just be thankful this new, outspoken Raina had shown up in his life just in time to sort through the mess he seemed to have found himself in.

"Let me ask you this. Why haven't you told her yet?"

"It may take a little while for Kitty to get used to the idea of being a stepmother."

"All the more reason to tell her now," she pointed out gently. "Waiting isn't going to make this any easier."

For the first time in days, Raina seemed like the Raina he was used to. Calm, levelheaded. Looking out for his best interests.

If he told Raina everything, she could help. This wouldn't be the first seemingly insurmountable problem she'd helped him solve.

But the last thing he wanted to do was admit the truth. It had taken years to coax a yes out of Kitty. Marrying her would seal the success of Messina Diamonds for decades to come. After all the years of work he'd put into it, he couldn't blow this deal.

"You have to tell her, Derek. And you have to do it the next time she calls. Or better yet, call her. You can explain not returning her phone calls before now, but if you wait even another day, she's going to just get more and more suspicious. She already thinks something is up. If you don't tell her soon, she'll dump you just for ignoring her."

"I know what I'm doing," he insisted.

"Not about this, you don't. Look, I'm sure you have a certain prowess with women…"

The tone of her voice, which implied she didn't believe that for a minute, set his teeth on edge.

"But this is different. Telling your fiancée you have an infant would tax the skills of Don Juan. Take the advice of a woman on this. She would rather know now."

Every instinct he had screamed that telling Kitty the truth would only make things worse. But what if he was wrong?

Relying on his gut had gotten him through innumerable business decisions. But relying on Raina was also second nature. In the nine years she'd worked for him, she'd never given him bad advice. Maybe her female intuition trumped his gut.

"Okay. I'll call her."

A tentative smile spread across Raina's face. "Thank God. Because she was driving me crazy calling me."

For an instant, she looked both young and unbelievably appealing. This new Raina drew him in a way the cool professional Raina never had. But which was the real woman?

Something tightened deep in his gut. With all his concern about Kitty, he couldn't help wondering if he was worried about the wrong woman.

As much as she didn't want to be alone with Derek at his house this morning, she wanted even less to be alone with Isabella. The tiny infant reminded her all too much of Derek.

She had the same intense blue-gray eyes, which slanted down at the outside corner in exactly the same way, giving her expression a sort of thoughtful intensity. Her hair was thick and curly, just like his, though her curls were a coppery-gold where his were dark brown and close-cropped into submission.

Only their mouths differed. Isabella's tiny rosebud

lips often parted in big toothless grins. Derek, on the other hand, almost never smiled, and when he did, never bared his teeth. It was an oddity she'd grown accustomed to. By now she was quite fond of his rare, close-mouthed smiles. Which somehow made it all the harder to see Isabella's generous, trusting grin.

Looking at the baby, Raina felt her heart constrict. Watching Isabella was like glimpsing another version of Derek himself. One who was less closed off. Less protective of himself.

Over the years they'd worked together, they'd spent countless hours together. He trusted her opinions. He'd discussed business goals and work strategies, but he'd never opened up to her. Not about anything personal. He'd never let her in.

But Isabella was different. Infants were born ready to love. They could bond with anyone who responded to their needs and paid them enough attention. How easy would it be to spend the next two weeks lavishing all her repressed love for Derek onto this tiny infant? How easy would it be to fall just as deeply in love with Isabella as she was with Derek?

All too easy. But for the health of her heart, it would be a mistake of catastrophic proportions.

No, the smart thing would be to keep her distance.

However, Isabella's gaze followed Derek as he left the room to call Kitty. She stared at the closed door to his home office through which he'd disappeared.

After a few seconds, she turned her head back and shot Raina a decidedly suspicious look.

Suddenly feeling defensive, Raina asked, "What?"

Isabella frowned, waving her arms about. Not the

cute batting at her toys she'd done when Derek was in the room, but in an annoyed, get-me-outta-here kind of way.

"It's no use getting mad at me. I'm not picking you up," Raina explained, squatting so she was at Isabella's eye level. "I'm just not doing it. You're cute enough as it is."

Isabella cocked her head to one side, listening intently. She held her arms up to Raina, her expression flashing from annoyed to pleading. When Raina didn't move, Isabella's lower lip began to tremble. Her wide blue-gray eyes filled with watery tears. A whimper of unspeakable sorrow escaped her lips.

Any second now, this kid was going to blow. She'd scream her head off. Derek would rush in, spot Raina's vulnerability and the deal would be off.

Faster than Raina could mutter, "Not on my watch," she'd leaned forward and extracted the ticking time bomb.

"Okay, kiddo, you win this round. Just don't give me away."

When Raina pulled Isabella into her arms, her tiny body shuddered with relief. She buried her face against Raina's neck, dampening her skin.

At the feel of that precious weight in her arms, something inside of Raina swelled, choking off her air supply and clogging her throat. An image flashed through her mind of the Grinch's heart expanding until it popped through the wire cage. She wanted to squeeze Isabella closer to her chest, to nuzzle the soft spot on the back of her neck, to relish the sensation of those tiny moist lips drooling on her.

And how sick was that?

She *wanted* baby drool? Had she completely lost her mind? This wasn't what she wanted. She wanted a life of her own. She wanted to go to culinary school. She wanted wire whisks and spring form pans. She wanted crème brûlée torches and chafing dishes.

She did not want to spend her days feeding mashed bananas to a drooly kid. She didn't care how cute she was.

Thrusting Isabella away from her, Raina held her at arm's length and met the girl's gaze. "Hold on there, Cindy-Lou Who. I'm not falling for this act. I've got younger siblings. I know for a fact you little ones can be sneaky as hell."

Isabella's tiny brow knitted in confusion. *What's not to love? What could I possibly do to be cuter?* she seemed to be asking.

"All I need from you is a little cooperation. I'm not the one you need to be charming. You need to send some of that cute Derek's way. Make him go all mushy inside."

If she didn't know better, she'd have sworn Isabella shrugged as if to say *What the hell.* Then she once again reached her arms out to Raina, her tiny fists opening and closing in a *gimme-gimme* motion.

Instinctively Raina pulled her close to her chest, this time bracing herself first for the rush of hormones that holding Isabella stirred up inside of her.

Pushing all the warm gooeyness aside, she tried to focus on the task at hand, considering what she could possibly teach Derek about being a father. Everything she knew about babies was pure gut instinct. It was nothing she'd learned from a book or an expert.

Isabella met her gaze, her blue-gray eyes wide and trusting.

"Kendrick used to look at me just like that," Raina murmured. Unbidden, an image of Kendrick as a baby drifted into her mind. "You remind me of him, you know. I was about eleven when he was your age. I thought I was the luckiest girl in the world. I didn't have to play with dolls, because I had a baby brother. All I ever wanted to do was play with him, feed him and cuddle with him. I couldn't wait to grow up and have a baby of my own."

Sadness washed over her as she felt a pang of loss deep within her soul. She'd wanted a family of her own so badly as a child. Then her father had left and suddenly helping with her brothers and sisters wasn't something she *got* to do, it was something she *had* to do. From the age of fourteen on, she'd picked up Lego blocks, wiped snotty noses and shuffled kids from one spot to another. When she'd left for culinary school at eighteen, she'd sworn off kids for life.

Then a scant year later, her mother had had a stroke, forcing Raina to walk away from her scholarship to help out at home. Which meant more snotty noses and mac 'n' cheese and checking homework. This time on top of a demanding job. She felt like she'd raised an army of kids, rather than just four.

Somewhere along the way her own dreams of motherhood had been buried under the dump truck full of responsibilities she'd been too young for. She felt much older than her twenty-eight years. Now, as she stood swaying back and forth with Isabella in her arms, sentimentality flooded her.

She remembered all her siblings at this age, even Lavender, who was only three years younger than she. Suddenly, it seemed as if the years had passed too quickly. How could she have known that one day she'd miss the hours she'd spent playing dolls with Cassidy? Or the slumber parties she'd planned for Jasmine and Lavender? Or the times when Kendrick couldn't sleep and she'd crawled into bed with him, cuddling his teddy bear between them as she told him stories until he'd fallen asleep?

How had she forgotten how wonderful those experiences were?

How had she forgotten how much she'd wanted children of her own, once upon a time?

And here was Isabella. This beautiful, perfect baby girl. The child of the man Raina loved. Innocent, vulnerable, and completely ready to love her in return. Ready to be lavished with attention and adored.

As Isabella cuddled closer to her chest, Raina felt tears prickle the backs of her eyes. She braced herself against a wave of yearning so profound it nearly brought her to her knees.

"But you're not mine," she murmured.

Falling in love with Derek's daughter would do her no more good than falling in love with him had done her. That had only led her to—as her mother would say—a heart-load of misery and a bucket of bad decisions.

Resolve hardened in her chest. Quitting her job at Messina Diamonds was the first step to a whole new life for her. If she won this bet with Derek and got the extra money from the severance package, plus the unemployment, she'd be free to go back to culinary school. To live the life she wanted.

As she felt Isabella squirm against her chest, guilt stirred in her heart. Which was ridiculous. She wasn't abandoning the child. Isabella wasn't hers to love. That was Derek's job. Raina just had to teach him to do it.

She would get Isabella to bond with Derek if she had to paint him with Gorilla Glue first.

She looked down at the cooper-haired little imp in her arms and muttered, "Okay, kiddo, prepare to fall in love with your daddy." Isabella's gaze narrowed with doubt. "Trust me, you just have to look past that cold facade of his. Once you see that underneath he's kindhearted and oddly vulnerable, you'll be a goner." *Just like I was.*

Before she could devise a more specific strategy than that, the door to Derek's office swung open. He stood there in the doorway, hands tucked into his pants' pockets, lips curved downward in a grim expression.

She met his gaze from across the room and for a moment wondered if he'd heard her comments to Isabella. That would certainly explain his forbidding expression. If there was one thing that made Derek uncomfortable it was having other people look past his exterior to see the man behind the executive.

However, when he spoke, she realized his unpleasant mood stemmed from something else entirely.

"We'll know soon enough if you were right about telling her the truth. Kitty is coming to Texas."

Five

He should have been thrilled with the news. The woman he'd spent years wooing, the woman who would guarantee the success of his company for years—if not generations—had finally been lured into visiting his home.

"You don't look pleased."

He brought his gaze up to meet Raina's. If he didn't look pleased, it was because he wasn't. Inexplicably, he didn't want to see Kitty. He didn't want her here.

"I'm thrilled," he said aloud.

"You don't sound thrilled."

"Trust me," he said grimly. "I couldn't be more excited."

He didn't bother to question why he was lying. It didn't take a genius to figure out why. Kitty was a beautiful, accomplished woman. The perfect complement to the life he'd built for himself. And less than two weeks after finally winning her, he'd found himself inexplicably attracted to Raina. A woman he'd known for nearly a decade and never before had a sexual thought about.

Obviously he wasn't genuinely attracted to Raina. This was merely his libido's stalling tactic. All the more reason to ignore every impulse he had about Raina. Especially the one stirred up by the image of her standing across the room, gently rocking his child in her arms.

She looked so natural holding his child, so right, that every instinct he had screamed at him to cross the room and pull her into his arms.

Instead he clenched his hands in his pockets and said, "In fact, the only thing that could please me more would be if by the time she arrived, Isabella was already comfortable with my company."

Again, he was lying, of course. He could think of a great many things that could please him more. A great many of them of involved stripping off Raina's T-shirt and exploring the delicate skin underneath it.

He spoke with such dry, humorless determination, she couldn't help quirking an eyebrow in question. His response was just so…well, so like him.

"Nothing could please you more?" she prodded. If he were still her boss—that is, if she was trudging along, being the dutiful employee—she'd let his bald-faced lie slide. But things were different now.

He looked at her without so much as a twitch to his expression. "What do you mean?"

"Frankly I can't tell what you're less excited about: having Kitty arrive or spending time with your daughter." Raina sauntered forward until she stood just before him, Isabella propped on her hip. "In nine years, I've never seen you approach a project with less enthusiasm. With less interest. With less pleasure. Therefore, you are most obviously not pleased about spending time with your daughter."

"Your point?"

She shook her head with mock sympathy for his ignorance. "Oh, come now, Derek. Surely even you can see the point I'm trying to make. This is your daughter. How exactly do you think your lack of enthusiasm makes her feel?"

Almost as if she'd been coached on her part, Isabella clutched her tiny fists in Raina's shirt and buried her face against her arm, as if desperate not to be passed over to Derek. Raina couldn't have asked for a better performance to make her point.

"She's five months old," Derek deadpanned. "I don't think she feels much of anything."

"Well, there's your problem."

"My problem."

She could tell from the complete lack of emotion in his voice that he was actually amused by their conversation. And furthermore, he was expecting her to share the joke. But the truth was, it all hit too close to home. So instead of amused, she just felt annoyed.

"Exactly. Your problem with Isabella. Is it any wonder she doesn't want to go into your arms, when you treat her as if she doesn't even have feelings?"

"She's five months old."

"And you don't believe five-month-olds have feelings?" Suddenly, they weren't just talking about Isabella anymore. Years of repressed feelings boiled up inside her. "Boy, that's classic Derek."

"What is that supposed to mean?"

She opened her mouth to speak, but everything that popped into her mind sounded irrationally angry. After all, was it really his fault that she'd stupidly fallen in love with him? No.

And no one had forced her to entertain countless fantasies in which he suddenly realized she was everything he desired. It certainly wasn't fair of her to blame him for not making her fantasies come true.

On the other hand, he may not have intended to, but he'd hurt her feelings. She felt his complete lack of awareness like a knife to the chest. How could she not be angry and frustrated by his ignorance?

Worse still, how could she explain any of this to him without revealing how vulnerable she was to him? How much she loved him?

So instead of responding, she snapped her mouth shut and clutched Isabella closer as she retreated into the kitchen.

For a moment, she simply stood there, relieved to be out from under his assessing gaze. When she heard him entering the kitchen behind her, she crossed to the cabinet and pulled out a glass. As she helped herself to water from the refrigerator door, she was all too aware of Derek behind her and the question hanging between them.

Suddenly the question felt much bigger than it should have. Which was her own damn fault. If she'd just answered him outright, he wouldn't realize how much her answer revealed.

Since he was still watching her, waiting for her answer, she sucked it up and spoke.

"Here's the thing, Derek. You put Messina Diamonds first."

"I do."

"Always. Without fail. Without question."

His gaze narrowed slightly. "What's your point?"

"You are so dedicated to Messina Diamonds, you never even consider what you might want. You completely suppress your own emotions because to you, they're just not important. And therefore, neither are anyone else's."

She watched him carefully, looking for signs of dawning realization. For some glimmer of understanding that for years she'd been pouring not just her time and energy into her job, but her heart into it, as well.

But instead of the flash of insight she'd expected to see, his jaw clenched. She'd pissed him off.

In nine years, she'd seen just about every emotion flicker across his face only to be quickly repressed. For him, anger wasn't yelling, ranting or—God forbid—anything as uncouth as throwing things. The maddest she'd ever seen him involved clenching his jaw, shoving his hands deep in his pockets and speaking in a very low voice. Which was exactly what he did now.

"I'm Messina Diamond's CEO. More people depend on me than you can possibly imagine. Therefore, what I want and need isn't important."

"More than *I* can possibly imagine?" she asked. "Don't think for a minute I don't know exactly how

many people you employ. I do know. And I know that
they depend on you. I know that the job you do is important. And don't get me wrong, your dedication is ad-
mirable."

It was, without a doubt, one of the things she most
admired about him. And probably—fool that she
was—one of the reasons she'd fallen in love with him
in the first place. But sadly, men completely devoted
to their work did not make good objects of affection.

"The problem is," she continued before he could in-
terrupt, "you work so hard to repress your own emotions
that you're convinced no one else has emotions, either.
But guess what, buddy, normal people—even five-
month-olds—have emotions. In fact, they're probably
far more sensitive to moods than most adults you deal
with."

Derek looked unconvinced. "So you're telling me
that it's my fault Isabella doesn't like me."

"I'm sorry to say it, but yes."

"Again. She's five months old. She can't even speak.
And if I had to hazard a guess, I'd say she doesn't
understand much, either."

"Exactly," she agreed. "If she can't understand what
you're saying, how do you think she knows how you
feel?"

"I'm guessing she doesn't."

"And that's where you'd be wrong. She knows what
you're feeling by watching your expressions, by listening to the tone of your voice. By looking in your eyes."

Derek looked skeptical. "You can't seriously expect
me to believe she can do all of that."

"You can believe whatever you want. I'm just telling

you what's been scientifically proven. One of the first skills infants learn is how to read moods and emotions. It's something Isabella is good at, regardless of whether or not you believe she's capable of it."

"But—"

"Hey, we can argue about this all day, if you want, but keep in mind you hired me to help with this precisely because you don't know anything about babies. So why not let me do the job you've hired me to do and teach you what I know?"

She infused as much confidence as possible into her voice and just prayed he wouldn't press her for details. The truth was she was just making stuff up. She had no idea whether or not anyone had scientifically proven infants could read emotions. But Raina knew in her heart it was true. Surely anyone who'd ever held a baby in their arms and gazed into her eyes would agree with her.

"If you don't believe me, just look at Isabella."

Derek's stony gaze dropped from Raina to his daughter. Isabella clung tightly to her shirt with her little face buried against Raina's neck. "What about her?"

"Normally, she's cheerful and charming. Because we're fighting, she's huddled against my chest. Clearly, she's picked up on our mood and is nervous."

"Okay," he said finally with a stiff nod. "Babies have emotions and are experts at reading them. Tell me how that helps me."

"Well, so far, it hasn't helped you at all. It's been working against you."

His jaw clenched again and for the first time that

day, she noticed the fine lines of exhaustion etched around his eyes. The sheer tension rolling off of him. She fought against the sympathy growing inside of her. This situation was his own damn fault. No one else would expect to bond emotionally with an infant in less than two weeks. No one else would expect their baby daughter to love them automatically. But Derek expected it. And he'd blame himself if it didn't happen.

She sighed, suddenly feeling as if she were kicking him when he was down. Still, she pressed on. "It's that emotion thing I was telling you about. You're very closed off. Very emotionally distant."

"Is this supposed to be helpful?"

She winced at the hint of pain in his voice. It wasn't impossible that her criticism had hurt his feelings. It just seemed so unlikely.

"Ultimately, yes, it should be helpful. You want to know why Isabella bonded so quickly with Dex?"

"Yes. That's exactly what I want to know."

She ignored the sarcasm in his voice. "She bonded with him so quickly because he fell in love with her right off the bat."

Derek all but smirked. "Dex fell in love with a baby?"

"Scoff all you want, I'm just telling you what I saw. You haven't seen it, because every time you're in the room with the two of them, all you can see is that your daughter likes him better. It's driving you crazy, so you don't see what's really going on there."

"I'm not a child, Raina. I'm not jealous of Dex."

Once again, it was all she could do not to bop him on the head, though this time the urge was tempered with amused exasperation. She shook her head ruefully. "Of course you're jealous of Dex."

He looked ready to argue with her, but she didn't give him the opportunity. He was so hard on himself, always so determined to do the right thing. And apparently, no one had ever told him it was okay to experience jealously.

"It's natural to feel jealous," she explained. "After all, you've pretty much succeeded at every thing you've ever done. You're simply not used to Dex excelling where you've failed."

"I wouldn't say he's excelled."

She rolled her eyes in exasperation. "I would. When he believed Isabella was his, he opened up to her. You should watch them together sometime. It's like he's a completely different person when he's with her. Well, her and Lucy."

She couldn't hide the note of wistfulness that crept into her voice as she was talking. Before Lucy had come into his life, she'd always thought of Dex as a little cold and impersonal. Never in a million years would she have pegged him as a candidate for uncle of the year, but in those few weeks he'd thought he was Isabella's dad, he'd been transformed.

Frankly, she was a little jealous herself. Not of Dex, but of Lucy, who had managed to win his heart. Of course, it wasn't Dex's heart Raina wanted. The Messina hearts were as complicated as they were well-guarded. Yet somehow Lucy had figured out a way in. Raina doubted she was even close to the right door.

Which was the kind of thinking that had made her so miserable during her tenure at Messina Diamonds.

And she couldn't help wondering, if in nine years working for him, she hadn't been able to get Derek to open up to her, how in the world was she supposed to get him to open up to Isabella in just two weeks?

Watching the emotions play across Raina's face, he could all but see her frustration mounting. So it didn't surprise him when she marched across the room and thrust Isabella back into his arms.

"Look, you want to bond with your daughter? Just talk to her."

As always, Isabella stiffened, holding her tiny body as straight as a rod of steal, her sturdy arms pressed against his chest with all her might. "Talk to her? About what?"

"Anything. Just let her hear your voice."

Staring into the face of his daughter, he finally admitted to Raina, "I don't know what to call her."

"Huh?" Raina asked, clearly baffled.

"I don't…" Normally he didn't have trouble explaining himself. But today, with Isabella and Raina, he felt crippling incompetence. "I don't have a name for her."

"Just call her by her name, Isabella. Or call her Izzie."

"Dex calls her Izzie."

Raina rolled her eyes. "But sure, you're not jealous of Dex. No, not at all." Raina glanced down at her watch. "Call her whatever you want to call her. Punkin', sweet pea, honeybun. Hell, call her rutabaga for all I care. Or, God forbid, follow in your brother's footsteps and call her Izzie. She does seem to like it. But I don't have time for this nonsense. I've got to go."

"But you just got here."

"Yes, and you asked me to clear your schedule for the next two weeks. Which means I've still got about fifty phone calls to make." She spun on her heel and marched toward his home office, leaving him staring from her to Isabella, unsure which female baffled him more.

Almost as if she sensed what he was about to say, Raina stopped at the office door and added, "And don't talk to her about work. Anything but business."

"As you've pointed out, work is my whole life. That doesn't leave much to talk about."

Raina shrugged nonchalantly. "Tell her something you've never told anyone. Something about your childhood."

When he continued to stare at her, waiting for inspiration to strike, she offered, "Childhood pranks? Amusing anecdotes? Misadventures? Anything? No?"

"That kind of crap was more Dex's style. I was too busy keeping the family together."

She sighed in a way that managed to sound both beleaguered and sympathetic. "I mean before your mom died. Before your father found those first diamonds. When your dad was still prospecting, you lived in ten different countries before the age of thirteen. You visited places most people have never even heard of. You had ample opportunity to stir up trouble. You had to have been a kid at some point. I refuse to believe that you were some serious-minded little version of yourself even then."

But he had been. Even then he'd known it was his job to make sure he and Dex were getting their education, no matter what country they lived in. When their mother died of cancer when he was thirteen, even more responsibilities had fallen on his shoulders. Keeping the family together was never something he resented. It was just what he did.

When he didn't answer, Raina propped her hands on her hips and glared at him. "Fine. You don't want to talk about your childhood? Tell her about your parents. Tell her about Dex. If all else fails, make something up. Just talk to her."

As Raina left, Derek could only shake his head in confusion. What was it she wanted from him?

Apparently when Raina had said he needed to "open up" to Isabella, she'd expected an outpouring of sentimentality. Or perhaps unresolved childhood angst. The truth was, he had no angst about his childhood.

Naturally, he'd been hard hit by his mother's death. They all had been. But they'd stuck together. He'd never resented the sacrifices he'd made for the family. He'd just done what needed to be done.

There was nothing to regret. At seventeen, not long after his father first discovered diamonds in Canada, Derek had taken over the business side of things for his father. He'd been cutting deals with men three times his age. He'd relished the challenge. And the truth was, he hadn't resented the sacrifice, because frankly, it had been a relief. Taking over the business from his father had finally given him a place in his freewheeling, fun-loving family.

In fact, right now, the only regret he could think of was that his assistant seemed to have morphed into someone else. Had she always been this passionate about things and he'd just never noticed? Or had she been completely suppressing her personality for the past nine years? Was he such a tyrant that she'd believed that necessary?

The phone rang halfway through dinner. Kendrick, ever the seventeen-year-old, jumped to answer it before Raina could remind him that at their last "family summit" they'd voted not to take phone calls during dinner.

A minute later he returned with the cordless handset in hand and a scowl on his face. "It's for you."

Cassidy slouched back in her chair, not bothering to shove aside her bleached blond bangs when they dangled in her eyes. "I thought Raina wasn't supposed to take calls from Darth Vader during dinner."

"No one is supposed to take calls," their mother pointed out diplomatically.

Raina shot her mother a grateful look as she accepted the handset. "Kendrick already answered it. I can't just hang up on him."

Cassidy glared at Kendrick, who merely poked at his stir-fry in response.

As she scooted her chair away from the table and left the room, Raina had no doubts about who was on the other end of the line. Four times in the past hour, her cell phone had rung, "The Imperial March" Darth Vader ring tone Kendrick had installed on her phone echoing through the kitchen before she'd finally switched her phone to vibrate. Her ambivalence about their conversation this afternoon made ignoring his calls all the easier.

When she'd left this afternoon, he'd seemed to be making progress. He'd mastered changing diapers and though Isabella didn't seem too happy about it, she'd even drunk the bottle Derek had heated up for her. Since he'd seemed stubbornly determined not to call the nanny for the night, she'd left believing Derek and Isabella would at least make it through the night. However the numerous phone calls had strained her optimism.

Two months ago, when her younger siblings had finally joined forces against "the Empire," she'd explained the new policy to Derek. Every evening between seven and eight, she'd be unreachable. Either he'd forgotten or was—once again—ignoring her attempts to set boundaries.

Once out of earshot of her family, she put the phone to her ear. "I thought you understood—"

"I know," he interrupted. "No phone calls during dinner."

"If you leave a message on my voicemail, I promise I'll—"

"But this is an emergency. I think Isabella has a fever."

She resisted the urge to scoff. "Look, Derek, kids get fevers all the time. Just take her temperature, if it's over—"

"How?"

"How, what?"

"How—" he spoke slowly with clipped words "—do I take her temperature?"

Ah. She'd forgotten she was dealing with a man who was both a control freak and knew zip about kids.

"First you've got to find the thermometer. Lucy is very thorough, so I'm sure she packed one in Isabella's bag. Then you'll need to take her temperature either rectally or under her arm."

"Rectally?" Derek's voice sounded choked.

"Yes. It's more accurate. And—" A chorus of complaints called out from the kitchen to protest her time on the phone. "Why don't you just look it up on the Internet like a normal person would. I'm sure there's a site somewhere that tells you how to take a kid's temperature."

Then, for the first time in nine years of working for Derek, she hung up on him.

Six

Frankly, it felt good. Though that single act of rebellion did little to mitigate her bruised emotions.

For all these years, she'd done everything he'd asked. She'd worked the long hours; she'd sacrificed her personal time. She'd defended him when others called him a tyrant and an unfeeling bastard. And she'd done it all because she'd believed she saw things in him no one else did. Because she believed they shared something he had with no one else. Even if he didn't love her—and she'd never had any illusions he did—she believed that he at least trusted and confided in her.

But it turned out, he was just clueless. He'd unwittingly broken her heart and she was just not ready to forgive him for that. Frankly, she wasn't even willing to let her stir-fry get cold.

"I should have done that years ago," she muttered as she pushed open the kitchen door, working hard to bury a twinge of guilt.

An hour later, as she was finishing up the dishes, she still wasn't entirely successful. She leaned toward Lavender, who was drying while she washed, and opened her mouth to speak.

"Stop obsessing."

Raina snapped her mouth closed. Then said, "I don't know what you're talking about."

"You're still worried that something is really wrong with Isabella. Just remember Derek is a competent adult. He'll figure it out. He's got to—"

Before Lavender could even finish her thought, the doorbell rang. A sinking feeling settled into her stomach. Lavender shot her an exasperated look.

"That better not—"

"Raina," Cassidy called from the living room. "It's for you."

Kendrick, without looking up from his homework, mimicked the heavy breathing of Darth Vader before giving in to a chuckle at his own joke.

Raina dried her hands and shot looks at both Lavender and Kendrick. "You two stay here."

Stifling her growing annoyance, she pushed through to the living room to find—just as she expected—Derek standing just inside the front door, a crying Isabella in his arms.

It was so disconcerting to see him standing there in her living room, for a moment she couldn't even speak. He was dressed much as he'd been earlier—the same dress pants and shirt, but he'd lost the jacket. The sleeves of his shirt had been rolled up. She'd seen him dressed just so many times, but always at the office, after hours. And he'd never before looked quite so…disheveled.

His hair was mussed as if he'd repeatedly run his fingers through it and something mysterious and beige stained his shirt.

Kendrick and Lavender hovered in the door behind her. Cassidy sat on the sofa beside their mother's wheelchair, watching a sitcom on TV. Acid poured into her stomach at the sight of their curious, appraising gazes. Given their playful—but genuine—animosity toward him, this had the potential to go very badly.

"You shouldn't have come," she told him.

He held Isabella out toward her. "I couldn't find the thermometer," he said accusingly, as if it were somehow her fault. "Then when I put her in the car to drive to the pharmacy to buy one, she started crying." He pulled an ear thermometer out of his pants pocket. "I bought this at the pharmacy, but every time I use it, I get a different reading. And she just keeps crying."

Lavender stepped around Raina and crossed the room. "That kind of thermometer is notoriously unreliable on infants," she said reassuringly as she held out her hands. "Here, let me take her."

Derek eyed her suspiciously.

"Derek, this is my sister, Lavender. She works parttime at a pediatrician's office."

"And I'm quite the expert temperature taker. We'll get this sorted out."

Reluctantly he released the crying Isabella into her arms. She quieted down almost instantly in Lavender's gentle touch. The two of them disappeared down the hall. The concern lining Derek's face didn't disappear so quickly.

She'd never seen him like this. He wasn't a man easily worried. If a problem arose, he fixed it. Simple as that.

But Raina knew all too well that the health of a loved one wasn't something you could fix. There were problems no amount of money or resolve could solve.

Raina's gaze automatically drifted in the direction of her mother. Though weak and confined to her wheelchair, her expression was as curiously eager as Cassidy's was.

"Derek, this is my mother, Rose Huffman." She hesitated before adding, "You may remember meeting her."

Derek jerked his gaze from the doorway through which Lavender and Isabella disappeared. "Yes. Of course. I remember."

Raina felt a blush creep into her cheeks. Of course he did. He had an excellent memory. Especially when it came to money.

He'd met her mother the first time she'd quit, eight years ago. At the time, her mother's health was still declining. She'd only just been confined to a wheelchair and their home was not yet handicap accessible. Raina had seen no option other than quitting her profitable job at Messina Diamonds to take another job that would allow her to work from home, where she could help care for her mother during the day.

Derek, however, had been unwilling to accept her resignation. He'd come to her home then, too. When he'd found out why she'd quit, he'd hired a construction crew to retrofit their tiny suburban home, giving Rose back her mobility and independence. He'd forbidden her from telling anyone in her family he was footing the bill. He'd insisted on calling it a bonus for making it through the first year.

His generosity had affected everyone in their home. When she'd thanked him profusely, tears pooling in her eyes, he'd merely cleared his throat and said, "Don't be ridiculous. You're the best assistant I've ever had. I'm not going to let you quit simply because the doors in your house were improperly sized."

That had been it. The very moment when she'd begun to love him. It had been all downhill from there.

And now, here he was, in her home once more and this time he was the worried one. Whatever annoyance she'd felt with him earlier in the day disappeared in the light of his current situation.

Since a display of sympathy was as likely to make him uncomfortable as her tears had all those years ago, she turned toward her family and began making introductions. "You already met Lavender, but this is my youngest sister, Cassidy. And Kendrick, my brother, is there by the door. My middle sister, Jasmine, is away at school."

Kendrick rushed forward, with his hand extended. "So, you're the diamond guy."

Derek shook Kendrick's hand automatically, but it took him a moment to refocus his attention. Finally he said, "Yes. I suppose I am."

"Cool." Kendrick scrubbed a hand over his spiky black flattop. "I've never met a billionaire."

"Kendrick," Raina chided. Kendrick may poke fun

of Derek, but he was as fascinated by wealth as any teenager.

She glanced toward her mother for backup, but Rose merely smiled, apparently unconcerned.

Derek blinked, either surprised or embarrassed, she couldn't tell which. She hoped he was surprised, because frankly she was embarrassed enough for everyone.

Kendrick ignored her. "So, Mr. Messina, do you have any advice to pass on?"

"Um…" Derek glanced in her direction. It may have been the first time she'd ever seen him at a loss for words. "Work hard and stay in school."

A nervous chuckle slipped forth from her lips.

"But," Kendrick pointed out, "didn't you drop out of school when your father discovered the site of the first Messina Diamond mine in Canada?"

"Kendrick!" This time it was Rose who protested. Apparently it was okay to grill guests, just not to bring up their lack of education.

"That's enough, Kendrick. Mr. Messina merely took the GED in lieu of graduating early. By then he was nearly finished with his course work anyway," Raina defended.

"No, Raina. It's fine."

Other than a momentary spasm of his jaw, Derek gave no indication that the question bothered him. Raina was sure it did though. No matter how many times she'd heard him field this question, his response was always the same.

"I would never recommend anyone drop out of school. I was extremely lucky things worked out as well for me as they did. And I certainly wouldn't have considered doing it if I'd had any other options."

"You mean, if your father hadn't just become a billionaire overnight."

Kendrick's tone was as respectful as his manner, but nevertheless, Raina heard the subtle insult in the statement. And could she blame Kendrick, for resenting—even a little—someone who appeared to have so much when they struggled just to get by? Of course, Kendrick didn't know all that Derek had done for their family.

Before Derek could respond, Raina leapt to his defense. "You forget, Kendrick, that finding diamonds doesn't make someone a billionaire overnight. Derek didn't drop out of school because he thought he'd never have to work again, he dropped out to help his father run the business."

She didn't want to say more in front of Derek for fear of offending him, but—as she understood it—his father may have been a brilliant geologist, but he'd never been much of a businessman. It the early days of Messina Diamonds, he'd made some pretty serious mistakes. If Derek hadn't stepped in to run the business side of things, the family would have lost everything.

He'd been just seventeen when he'd taken over for his father. He'd missed most of his last year of high school. He'd never gone to college. Who knew what else he'd missed out on. After all, Messina Diamonds had become his whole life. He'd been working eighty-hour weeks since he was seventeen. He may be a billionaire, but she wouldn't let anyone imply he hadn't worked for it.

She gave Kendrick a heavy pat on the back. "I believe you still have a calculus test to study for."

"But—"

"And if tomorrow you're still interested in Derek's business history, I'm sure I can dig up some press releases for you read."

Steering Kendrick toward the kitchen, she gave a sigh of relief when Lavender emerged from the hall carrying a silent and very tired-looking Isabella.

"She's fine," Lavender announced. "Temperature's normal. She probably just felt hot to you because she's dressed warmly. Then she probably got fussy because you woke her up and wouldn't stop messing with her."

Derek's cheeks flushed with apparent embarrassment as he held out his arms for Isabella.

Lavender didn't hand her over. "I've almost got her back to sleep. Why don't you let me carry her out to the car for you? Then at least she'll sleep through the drive home."

He shoved his hands in his pockets and nodded stiffly. Raina knew that Lavender was only trying to help, but suspected she'd just made things worse. Derek wasn't a man who liked asking anyone for help. Having to come here at all had to rankle him. Now, to top it off, he undoubtedly thought Lavender was implying he'd done everything wrong.

Lavender, unaware of the insult she'd just delivered, strolled out to his car, gently rocking Isabella and humming a little tune. After Derek apologized to Rose for interrupting their evening, Raina and Derek followed.

Raina noticed for the first time that Derek was driving Dex's SUV rather than his own. "Still haven't moved

Isabella's car seat over to your SUV, huh?" His only
response was a beleaguered glance that made her wish
she hadn't brought it up. "Don't worry, we'll do it
tomorrow."

While Lavender lingered by the car, swaying
Isabella to sleep, Raina placed her hand on Derek's
arm, halfway down the path.

He turned to her, his expression still troubled in the
half-light of dusk. Pulling his keys from his pocket he
beeped the door unlocked with his remote.

As they stood, waiting for Lavender to ease Isabella
into the car seat and get her buckled, Raina forced a
wry chuckle. "And now you see why I work so hard to
keep my work life and my personal life separate."
Derek turned his gaze to her, his expression blank. "I
apologize for Kendrick's behavior," she explained.
"He's not used to being in polite company."

A glimmer of understanding lit in Derek's eyes. "I
doubt Kendrick considers me polite company."

"I don't know what you mean." But her protest
sounded lame, even to her.

Derek's lips twitched into a half smile. "Oh, come
on. The ring tone for my number on your cell phone?
You didn't think I ever noticed? Dum dum dum, Dum
de dum, Dum de dum. That's the theme music for some
famous bad guy. Was it the Terminator?"

She buried her face in her hands. Cringing, she admitted, "No, it's Darth Vader. But how…"

"Did I know that was Kendrick's idea? You'd mentioned he gave you all new ring tones for Christmas
last year."

"Ah." She lowered her hands and forced herself to

look at him. "I'm sorry. My family can be a bit irreverent. And I never dreamed you would notice."

"Maybe I pay better attention than you think." His voice was soft and low, like a caress. His words a balm to soothe her frayed emotions.

The intensity of his gaze shot through her, heating her blood and weakening her knees. She sucked in a deep breath as awareness stretched between them.

She felt herself swaying toward him as if the earth were shifting beneath her feet. Then he reached up his hand to brush aside a lock of her hair.

"There's no need to apologize," he murmured.

She was so lost in the potential of the moment, it took her a second to respond. "They don't mean anything by it. They're just—"

"It's okay."

"It isn't," she protested, and she wasn't talking only about her siblings' teasing, but also about the tension growing between her and Derek. She forced herself to step away from him. "I should have put a stop to it years—"

"Raina, it's fine." As if he sensed the change in her, his tone darkened.

"But they have no idea how much you've done for us. And I—"

This time Derek pressed a finger to her lips, halting her protests. "Apparently you don't think I can take a joke."

The warmth of his finger against her mouth stifled any urge she had to continue arguing with him. Heat surged through her, stirring desires she thought she'd long ago suppressed.

She wasn't supposed to feel this way. She was supposed to be getting over him. So why wasn't she?

Glancing away to avoid his gaze, she noticed Isabella was now sleeping peacefully in her car seat. Lavender had apparently slipped inside without Raina even noticing. That happened sometimes when Derek was around—everyone else just faded into the background.

She was suddenly struck by the intimacy of being alone with him on a darkened street. Of standing so close beside the car. There was something illicit about it. Something that harkened back to teenage dates, to spending the last few minutes before curfew parked in the driveway, necking with her boyfriend in the front seat of his car.

She forced herself to step away from him, to pick up the dangling thread of the conversation. "I guess I *didn't* think you'd have a sense of humor about this."

He shrugged, casting her a wry smile. "It could be worse. They could call me Norman Bates."

She chuckled at the image and the awareness she'd felt earlier morphed into something new. "Somehow I just can't see you nursing an obsession with your dead mother. It's an entirely too spineless a form of villainy."

"But you can see me ruling the evil empire?"

"Yes," she joked. "I think that's kind of the point." Then her smile faded and she shook her head. "No. Honestly, I can't. If my family knew about all you'd done for them, they'd feel differently. And you can't tell me it doesn't hurt your feelings just a little bit."

He shrugged, stepping into the car. "I've never much cared what people thought about me. I have a job to do.

I do it. That job doesn't entail winning popularity contests or having people like me."

She let his comment slide, watching him shut the door and drive away, without pressing the issue. But once he was gone, she couldn't help wondering about his comment about popularity contests. Somehow, that's exactly what he'd set between him and Dex. A popularity contest. With Isabella as the judge.

And contrary to what he'd said, she couldn't help but believe he would in fact be very disappointed if he found out Isabella didn't like him.

Disconcerted by the wave of protectiveness that thought stirred up, she turned her thoughts to the other big revelation of the evening.

So Derek not only had a sense of humor, but a self-deprecating one to boot? How unexpectedly appealing. How completely delightful that he could still surprise her after all these years. How completely disastrous for her plans to excise him from her heart.

Just when her anger was allowing her to build more walls around her heart, how dare he find new ways to sneak around them?

Seven

Infant car seats had to be part of a vast government conspiracy to drive otherwise sane, intelligent adults absolutely batty. Derek could see no other reasonable explanation for why they would be so damned hard to install.

Of course, the car seat couldn't be blamed for his current emotional state. Raina was responsible for no small part of his frustration. He'd planned to spend their time together convincing her to stay with Messina Diamonds. Instead, for the past three days, she had him buried in dirty diapers and pink frilly dresses. He'd never in his life felt so incompetent. Until he'd decided to install this damn car seat.

He'd be tempted to chuck the blasted thing down the driveway and into the road, except Kitty was arriving from New York this afternoon. Derek had every intention of meeting her at the airport, with Isabella.

Isabella was a cute kid. Even he, with his complete lack of baby experience, could see that. For nearly a week now he'd watched her charm Raina into submission. One look at those long-lashed blue eyes of Isabella's and surely Kitty would fall in love with the little imp. Derek was counting on it.

"How's it going?" Raina's cheerful voice asked from outside the car.

Derek currently knelt in the backseat of his Lexus RX hybrid, head ducked, spine twisted, back hunched and seconds away from spasming. Beads of sweat formed on his upper lip and plastered his shirt to his back, despite the fact that he'd parked his SUV in the shade of live oaks lining his driveway.

For the hundred and tenth time, he shoved the patented, easy-secure latch into the crevice of the seat, praying that this time he'd hear the "click" described in the owner's manual. And for the hundred and tenth time, when he tugged on the strap, the latch pulled free.

He muttered a string of curse words, most of which he hadn't said aloud in decades.

"What did you say?" she asked.

He sucked in a deep breath. *Time Magazine* had once called him "the most successful CEO under 30." *Business Weekly* had described him as "a brilliant strategist." Hell, he'd been rated one of Dallas's most eligible bachelors five years running. So how the hell had he been outsmarted by a damn car seat?

Aloud, he said, "It's going great."

No way was he going to admit that this was yet another arena of fatherhood at which he was failing miserably.

"Are you sure? Because I've heard they can be kind of tricky."

Kind of tricky? He'd have gone with conniving. Or devious. Or evil incarnate.

He shot a look over his shoulder to find Raina just behind him, bobbing up and down, angling to see over his shoulder. When she realized she'd been caught, she bit down on her lip with a grin and shrugged her shoulders. The mischievous gleam in her eyes tugged at something deep inside of him.

He was seeing yet another side of her. One that was playful and mischievous. Man, what he wouldn't give to see that expression over a bowl of strawberries and whipped cream. It was the stuff of fantasies.

Fantasies which were, at the moment, strictly forbidden.

The weather had turned unseasonably warm overnight. When Raina showed up at his house this morning, instead of the jeans and T-shirt she'd worn the day before, she'd been clad in denim shorts and a green tank top.

There was nothing wrong with her clothes. Her shorts weren't too short, despite the tempting length of leg they revealed. Her tank top was modestly cut, covering everything that needed covering, even if it did cling to her breasts in a manner entirely too appealing. However, on her, the outfit seemed downright suggestive.

Which might have been more bearable if she wasn't

hovering. Eager to help, she trotted around to the other side of the SUV and climbed in. She shot him a sympathetic look over the car seat.

"Let me help. You've been at this for a while now. I'm guessing you need a break."

"Where's Isabella?"

"I rocked her to sleep and put her down in the bouncing seat in the living room." Raina patted the receiver to the baby monitor she had clipped to her hip. It squealed static in response. "I'll hear if she wakes up."

"Great," he muttered. Just great. He'd worked for hours last night trying to get Isabella to sleep. Raina did it in less than thirty minutes.

She tilted her head to the side with a frown as she studied his face. "And you look exhausted. How late were you up with her last night?"

He felt a growl of annoyance rumbling through his chest and snapped, "Late."

"Ah. I thought so. Maybe you should call Mrs. Hill again for tonight." When he glared at her, she held up a hand. "Or not. If you really feel like you have to do everything for yourself or you're a failure, then by all means, work yourself into a state of exhaustion."

Then, with quick efficiency, she nudged his hands out of the way and began loosening all the straps. "Did you read the instruction manual?" she asked as she plunged one of the latches between the seat back and base.

"Of course I read the manual." Briefly. "You're supposed to hear a—"

And at that moment, she wiggled her hand around and the latch gave a loud click as it snapped into place.

"A click?" she asked with a grin.

Smiling at him from over Isabella's car seat, she looked so impertinent, so unlike the Raina he knew, he was struck by the sudden notion that maybe he hadn't known her at all.

Was that possible? Had he really worked side by side with this woman for nearly a decade and not actually seen her? He'd sure as hell never noticed how attractive she was. How tempting.

Had he disappeared so completely into his role as CEO that he'd stopped seeing people for who they really were? And did it matter, when no one saw him beyond his position anyway?

Crouching, Raina wiggled around the car seat to his side of the car. He had to climb out to make room for her, and still she seemed to fill the entire backseat. As thin and willowy as she was, her arms and legs seemed everywhere, brushing against him as she maneuvered into place. She snapped in the second latch, then wiggled around again so her knee was lodged in the car seat.

"I read somewhere that the only way to really get these straps tight enough is to put your weight in the seat." She sounded slightly out of breath, no doubt from all the wiggling.

But to him, the sound was positively erotic. That combined with the tempting view she'd presented him with of her behind made his senses leap to life. The fog of his exhaustion lifted as sexual awareness prickled along his nerve endings.

Finally, she scooted back to the other side of the car and shoved at the car seat. "There you go. Doesn't move more than an inch in any direction. It's perfect."

Her cheeks were flushed with exertion and delicate beads of moisture dotted her forehead as her breath continued to come in short bursts. His body responded automatically to the tempting picture she presented. *This was how she'd look after climaxing.*

That's when it hit him. He wanted her. This wasn't some passing whim. As inconvenient as it was, all he could think about was stripping off those shorts of hers, pulling those mile long legs around his waist and burying himself in her heat. *Damn it.*

"Perfect."

At his growl, she chuckled knowingly. "Except that I did it for you and you're still bound and determined to do this all by yourself, aren't you? Got to maintain that all important control, right?" Bending over the seat, she gave a sigh of exaggerated exasperation. With a series of clicks, she released each of the latches and sat back. "Okay, I'll talk you through it as you do it."

For a moment, he merely stared at her. How could she be so immune to the tension between them? Yet she seemed completely unaware he wanted to haul her across the seat and kiss her senseless then strip off her clothes and explore the silken skin of her lithe thighs.

But since she was staring at him expectantly, he loosened the straps of the car seat like he'd seen her do, and gave it another shot.

He rammed the latch back into the space between the seats, this time jamming his finger. He cursed again, loudly enough that she couldn't help hearing.

He sat down on the bench seat, swinging his legs around so they hung out the open car door. Raina winced sympathetically, which only made him scowl more.

"Let me see it."

Before he could protest, she'd stepped forward so she was standing between his legs. She'd pulled her hair back into some sort of ponytail, which bobbed in loose honey-blond curls against the back of her neck as she moved.

She took his hand in both of hers and turned it palm up on his leg, so that the backs of her hands rested against the top of her thigh. Her touch was painstakingly gentle. Her hands warm and dry against his. Her fingers both delicate and long.

He opened his mouth to tell her that she had the wrong hand, but as he did so, he sucked in a breath of air filled with her scent. The words he'd been about to say evaporated and he snapped his mouth shut.

How in the world had he worked beside her for so long and never noticed how appealing she smelled? Delicately feminine and fresh. Like a warm spring day. Like mischief and playing hooky. Like temptation itself.

"You shouldn't be so hard on yourself," she chastised gently. "Car seats are notorious for being difficult to install. That's why some people take workshops on how to do it. And why people take them by the fire department to make sure they did it right."

And all the while, she rubbed her thumbs across his palm and up his finger, applying light pressure. No doubt waiting for him to wince in pain, still unaware she had the wrong hand. Her touch was so soothing and gentle, soon his finger wasn't the only thing throbbing.

"The car seat isn't what's frustrating me."

Her gaze darted to his. Her eyes were wide, her pupils dilated. She sucked in a deep breath as awareness sparked between them.

Ah. So he wasn't the only one affected. He reached a hand out, but she deftly stepped away from his touch.

"I still remember how mad my dad got trying to install Kendrick's car seat."

Her tone was bright and cheerful. Exactly as it had been all morning long. Overly cheerful, he now realized.

"Raina—"

But she ignored him and continued talking. Babbling nervously. "I must have been about eleven, and I remember standing in the doorway of the garage watching him. I'd never heard anyone cuss so much. Gosh, I haven't thought about that for years."

Her voice trailed off. When he looked up, her brow was knitted into a frown and her eyes held the saddest expression.

Funny, he'd always thought of her as being coolly professional. Almost distant. And yet, watching this mixture of sorrow and confusion drift across her face, he realized now that he was used to seeing her cheerful. Not ebullient or giddy, just sort of quietly happy. Now, she wasn't, and he didn't know if he was to blame or the memory of her father was.

Staring blankly down at his hand, she murmured. "That was years before he left. I'd forgotten that he was unhappy even then."

The gentle yearning in her expression tugged at something deep inside of him. She blinked and a single tear slipped free of her eye to trail down her cheek.

Without thinking, he reached up and brushed away the tear. She blinked again, this time in surprise. He felt her sharp intake of breath against the back of his hand.

Part of him knew that if he stopped to consider what he was doing he'd recognize what a very bad idea this was. But he didn't give himself time to think. For the first time in years, decades probably, he didn't rationalize a decision. He didn't think it through. He didn't consider all the angles, all the advantages and disadvantages. He just acted.

He slipped his hand behind her head and pulled her closer to him. She stepped farther between his legs, closing the distance between them.

He'd meant to simply comfort her. And yet, when he leaned forward, pulling her mouth to his, comfort was the last thing on his mind. All he wanted was to explore her mouth. To taste her lips and somehow snatch some of the precious warmth for himself.

Her lips were soft beneath his. Her kiss impossibly sweet. Full of delicious innocence.

The hesitancy of her touch—the faint tremble in her hands as her fingers crept up his thighs—ratcheted up his desire. Suddenly, the need to offer comfort vanished, only to be replaced by true passion. By the need to possess.

His tongue pushed past her lips, plunging into her mouth, only to be met by her own, stroke for stroke. He buried his hands in her hair, tugging at her ponytail until it pulled loose and her hair tumbled over his hands.

Any ability he might have mustered to resist her was completely destroyed by the fervency of her response.

She was liquid fire in his arms. A molten explosion of pure passion. Even knowing it was a mistake to keep kissing her, he didn't care. Didn't care that kissing her would only make things worse. Would only make him want things he couldn't have. For the moment, the only thing that mattered to him was the heat of her mouth under his, the touch of her hands on his thighs. The press of her body against his.

He briefly considered leading her into the house, upstairs to his bedroom, but he dismissed the idea. His exclusive Highland Park neighborhood wasn't the type where people fooled around in their cars, but he'd parked by the side of the house and they were well hidden from the street. No one would see them. No one would know. And he wouldn't have to decide to break the vow implicit in his engagement to… What was her name? What did it matter when Raina's hands were inching up his thighs?

He matched her, move for move, dropping his hands to her waist, to explore the delicate skin just above her waistband. Her stomach muscles leapt at his touch, trembling against his palm. He could feel her rib cage vibrating as she struggled to suck in air. His hand inched toward her breast. He'd just cupped its delicious weight when Raina jumped. Not with anticipation.

She literally leapt away from him, putting a good three or four feet of distance between them in a single movement. She spun from him, facing the line of live oaks that bordered his drive, burying her face in her hands.

Confusion rocketed through him. One moment she'd been in his arms, hot and eager, the next she was jumpy and distraught. What the hell had he done? Why had she…

A full moment had passed before he heard the clatter of footfall on the driveway. By the time he looked up, Kitty Biedermann was rounding a curve in the path.

Raina had to hand it to her. Kitty Biedermann had impeccable timing. A few minutes later and she might have discovered Raina and Derek naked in the back of his car. A few minutes earlier and she would have interrupted nothing at all.

As it was, Raina had heard her strolling up the drive just in time to jump guiltily out of Derek's arms. Just in time to ruin the perfect kiss Raina had dreamed about countless times over the past few years.

Just in time to make her feel like the other woman. Dirty and shameful.

If anyone should feel shameful, it was Derek. He's the one who'd kissed her, not the other way around. However, when she'd steadied herself by brushing her hair back from her face and turned to glance at him, she found him leaning calmly against his SUV, his gaze guarded, his hands tucked into his pockets.

Resentment spiked through her. How dare he look so unaffected by their kiss? How dare he apparently feel not even a glimmer of guilt?

To avoid looking at Derek if nothing else, Raina turned toward Kitty, who'd stopped maybe ten feet away from Derek and the SUV. She wore a thin black skirt and blazer. Her feet were clad in the kind of spiky pumps that cost more than a semester of Cassidy's college. Kitty's sable hair fell sleekly to her shoulders.

On Raina the outfit would have looked ridiculously mannish. Kitty, however, looked like a modern Lauren Bacall, curvy and outrageously sensual. Compared to Kitty, Raina felt like a twelve-year-old girl.

A cheating, shameful twelve-year-old girl. Perfect.

"You're early." Derek was the first to break the silence.

"I caught an earlier flight." Kitty wrinkled her perfectly straight nose. "No sense waiting around at the airport, is there?"

She lifted her hand to her sunglasses and slowly raised them onto the top of her head. The better to survey her domain. Her gaze flickered dismissively from Derek to Raina before settling on the house, which sprawled over the meticulously landscaped grounds. "Well. It's certainly large, isn't it?" Somehow she made that, too, sound like an insult. Finally, her gaze moved back to Raina. Again her nose wrinkled as she looked Raina up and down, taking in the shorts and tank top, so practical in the heat, but so pedestrian compared to Kitty's ensemble. "And you are…the dog walker? The nanny?"

Raina clenched her hands into fists. "Derek's assistant."

Kitty's gaze darted to Derek's. "Really? You've hired a teenager as your personal assistant?"

Finally Derek straightened—apparently no longer struck dumb by the sheer joy of unexpectedly seeing his lovely fiancée… "Raina is my administrative assistant at work. She's just helping out with Isabella this week."

"Ah." Kitty eyed her. "So, Louraina, you've been

demoted to nanny?" Kitty smirked. "And the child? Where is she?"

"Isabella is asleep. Finally." Derek crossed to Kitty's side and—to Raina's horror—brushed a kiss across her lips. "I'm thrilled you're here. But you really should have called to let me know you'd made that earlier flight. I'd planned to pick you up at the airport myself." He gestured behind him to the discarded cardboard box the car seat had come in. "I was just putting the car seat in so that I could bring Isabella with me."

Kitty waved a dismissive hand. "I hired a limo at the airport. It was much more convenient than having you pick me up." The disdainful look she shot the car seat box implied it was actually more convenient than traveling with Isabella.

Then she shot an equally scornful look at Raina. "The limo driver should be bringing up my bags. Tip him, will you?"

Then Kitty threaded her arm through Derek's and strolled up the winding walkway toward the house, concisely dismissing Raina. Relegating her to nothing more than the hired help.

And Derek let her lead him away.

Raina's stomach rolled over in disgust. Okay, so technically, it wasn't "into the sunset" since it was only about two in the afternoon, but metaphorically, the credits had already started to roll.

"Good riddance," she muttered. And she even almost meant it.

"Excuse me, miss, where do you want the bags?"

Raina spun around to find the limo driver rolling a

shoulder-high stack of luggage up the drive. Not one but two hanging bags were hung over his shoulder. The guy looked all of nineteen and maybe a hundred and twenty pounds. Raina figured the luggage probably had a good forty pounds on the kid, because he'd had to wedge his shoulder against it to push it up the hill.

"Oh, for goodness sake," she said, as she watched the driver wheeze his way toward her.

"The bags…" he puffed. "Where do…you want… them?"

"I suppose the bottom of White Rock Lake is out of the question."

He looked at her blankly. Probably because he didn't get the joke, but possibly because he was about to pass out.

She took pity on him. "On the doorstep is fine." Then she realized he'd have to hand carry each of the six—or was it seven?—bags up the flagstone walkway to get to the porch. "No, never mind. Here is fine. Her fiancé can bring them the rest of the way."

The word "fiancé" curdled on her tongue. And to think, mere minutes ago her tongue had been involved in such pleasurable activities.

Warmth flooded her as she relived the feel of his lips on hers. His kiss had been everything she'd ever dreamed. It had been a kiss designed to dominate. To sweep aside objections and banish doubts. In that moment, nothing had mattered but their desire. In that moment, she'd have willingly sold her soul for more of his touch. Fool that she was.

Well, it served her right. What had she been thinking, kissing another woman's fiancé? That had *bad idea* written all over it. Had her common sense taken a sabbatical? Had her morals abandoned her completely?

For nine years she'd known Derek when he hadn't been engaged and she waited until *now* to kiss him? What an idiot.

Though in her defense, he'd kissed her first. He'd started it. And he was the one who was so gaga over the lovely Ms. Biedermann. What was up with that?

"You sure this is okay, miss? 'Cause I can take 'em the rest of the way up."

Only then did she realize she was scowling at the poor limo driver. He'd hefted two of the bags off already, and held the third poised in the air, awaiting her command. She sighed and forced a friendly smile. "It's great. Just perfect."

A few minutes later, as she fished a twenty out of her own wallet to tip him, she couldn't help wondering, was Kitty Biedermann really as bad as she seemed? Or did Raina just feel guilty for kissing her fiancé?

Either option was unpleasant.

She'd never been that kind of woman. She didn't poach. It just wasn't her style.

And she vowed it would never happen again. The past few days she'd fallen into an oddly informal routine with Derek. Circumstances alone had led to this disaster. Well, circumstances combined with years of repressed desire. But that was all over with. Just because she'd cast aside her professional clothes for the two-week stint helping out with Isabella, that did not mean she'd cast aside her morals.

Derek was off-limits. Permanently. And if her libido didn't like it, it could just go throw itself in White Rock Lake.

Eight

Clearly, kissing Raina had been a bad idea. Even if he hadn't almost been caught by Kitty, it would have been disastrous. How exactly was he supposed to go about the business of pretending to be enthusiastic about Kitty's visit when what he wanted most was another woman? However, if he did a piss-poor job of pretending to be happy to see her, Kitty seemed not to notice. Nice thing about dating an heiress, he supposed. Kitty was generally so busy making sure people heard what she said, she rarely listened to anyone else.

As soon as they'd entered the house, she'd left his side. As he watched her move about his home, he tried to muster some enthusiasm for her. She was, as he told himself over and over again, the very embodiment of everything he'd ever wanted in a spouse. She had a poised elegance that surpassed mere beauty—though she certainly was beautiful. However, her looks hadn't been what drew him to her. It was more than that—the way her presence commanded attention. And yet, the very thing that he'd always admired about her was oddly unappealing today.

Now, she strolled from room to room as if she owned the place—and indeed, someday she would— her gaze appraising and cold.

"I suppose it isn't bad. After all, you can't be expected to have the kind of elegance you'd find on the Upper West Side, now can you? I'm sure your decorator was very competent. For Dallas."

Derek gritted his teeth against a response. He'd hired the best decorator in the state. She'd worked on the house, personally, for nearly a year. When she'd finished it had been featured in not one, but three respected magazines. The house had a cool elegance he'd never been comfortable in, but it wasn't about comfort. It—and its address—were physical evidence that he'd made it. No one would dream of dismissing a man who owned a seven-million-dollar home in Highland Park.

But if he had to spend another million dollars to have it decorated to his fiancée's taste, then so be it.

When she glanced his way, he forced himself to concede. After all, it was just furniture. He didn't give a damn what she did with it. "Of course you'll feel free to hire the decorator of your choice."

She smiled with benign indulgence. Then she crossed back to his side and patted him on the cheek dismissively. "We'll see."

An unpleasant implication hung in the air between them, but before he could figure out what she meant, the front door swung open and Raina swept into the entry hall. She held in her hand a carry-on tote, which she dropped unceremoniously by the front door.

"I had the driver leave the bags by the walkway to save him the trip. Someone should go get them." Raina's smile was overly bright.

Kitty didn't even turn around to acknowledge Raina's presence.

With a sigh, he left Kitty's side and headed out for the bags. When he passed close to Raina and might have spoken to her, she beat him to the punch.

"You owe me the twenty I tipped the driver."

Her tone was cold and unapproachable. He couldn't blame her. By kissing her today, he'd royally screwed up in a way he hadn't in years.

Not only had he jeopardized his relationship with Kitty, but he'd also ruined any chance he had of convincing Raina to stay on as his assistant. Even if he could lure her into staying, doing so would be a disaster. Now that he'd held her in his arms, he'd never forget the feel of her lips under his. He'd never stop wanting her. Which meant he had to let her go completely.

He'd picked Kitty. If he was having second thoughts now, that was his own damn fault. He certainly didn't need to drag Raina into things.

Yet somehow the only thing worse than the idea of marrying Kitty was the idea of never kissing Raina again.

Raina stood awkwardly in the doorway leading from the entryway to the living room, watching Kitty.

She'd never in her life felt more out of place. More out-classed.

As a rule, she wasn't given to fits of insecurity. The way she saw it, she was what she was. A girl from a lower-middle-class family who worked hard for a living. When she'd first taken the job at Messina Diamonds, she'd thrust herself professionally—if not socially—into a stratosphere of wealth and privilege she'd never before imagined. She'd had to work to blend in to that world, not because it was what she desired, but because it was her job. Though very few people she associated with through work would guess her humble beginnings, she'd never been ashamed of who she was or where she came from.

Next to Kitty Biedermann's glamour, she felt plain, drab and working-class. Like Mary Ann outshone by Ginger, the movie star. Her initial impulse—to slink quietly away—sat unpleasantly in her belly until she squashed it altogether.

Kitty may be Derek's fiancée, but this wasn't her turf yet. Raina still had the home-field advantage. At least for another week or so until Derek fired her. Until then, she wasn't going to give an inch to this obnoxious, pretentious drama queen.

By the time Kitty finished observing her future domain, Derek had returned from carting her luggage upstairs.

Without so much as a glance at Raina, he told Kitty, "I've put your luggage in the guest room at the top of the stairs. You can't miss it."

Kitty opened her mouth as if to protest, but with an unhappy glance in Raina's direction, she snapped it closed again. Her lips settled into a pout, but she nodded.

The message had been clear. He wasn't yet sleeping with Kitty.

Was that supposed to make Raina feel better?

Because it didn't. Guilt chased jealousy as it burned its way through her belly. Derek wasn't hers to kiss.

Of course, she'd known that from her first conversation with Kitty. But knowing about Kitty and being faced with the reality of Kitty were two completely different things.

Raina hated the idea of being chased away. But not as much as she hated the idea of watching them together.

"You know what," Raina said. "I'm just going to skadoodle out of here. Get out of your wa—"

"No." Derek's response was firm and instantaneous.

The look of surprised annoyance that Kitty sent him had to equal her own, not that Raina took any reassurance in that.

"Really, Derek dear," Kitty cooed as she draped herself around him. "Wouldn't you rather be alone?"

Every cell in Raina's body recoiled from the sight of Kitty's curves plastered against Derek. It was wrong. Repulsive even. Like the embalmed two-headed snake her science teacher had shown them in the ninth grade.

Raina didn't give Derek a chance to answer. If he wanted to be alone with Kitty, Raina certainly didn't want to know about it.

Besides which, if she had to watch them together for much longer, she may well do something she regretted. Like puke all over Kitty's designer pumps. "Obviously, now that Kitty is here, my presence is unnecessary."

"I disagree." Though he stood beside Kitty, one arm carelessly about her tiny waist, Raina felt the full force of his attention. "Unless you want to break our agreement, you've still got more than a week of helping me with Isabella."

"Ah," Kitty purred. "So she *is* the nanny."

Raina didn't waffle for an instant. Kiss or no kiss, Kitty or no Kitty, she still had every intention of winning her bargain with Derek. Ignoring Kitty's gleeful jab, she bumped up her chin and faced Derek head on.

"Of course I'm not breaking our agreement. I merely thought that with Kitty here, you wouldn't need me." He didn't so much as flinch. So she narrowed her gaze and pushed a little harder. "After all, you can imagine how much I'd hate being a third wheel."

Derek clenched his jaw, a sure sign he'd gotten her meaning and was trying hard not to let his irritation show. "You're still my employee. And the last time I checked, you work eight-hour days."

"Eight?" she scoffed. Ten to twelve was more like it.

He ignored her. "Besides, Kitty here is probably tired from her trip and will want to rest."

Being dismissed was apparently too much for Kitty. She pulled herself from his grasp and propped her hands on her hips. She didn't stomp her foot in protest, but Raina got the impression she wanted to.

"Honestly, Derek. Just let the nanny go home."

"She's not the nanny."

"I'm not the nanny."

She and Derek spoke at the same time, clearly equally annoyed with Kitty. For just an instant, her eyes met his. His lips gave the slightest twitch as if Kitty's fit amused him. Loss tightened around Raina's heart as tears prickled unexpectedly at the backs of her eyes.

She'd miss this. These moments of synchronization, of knowing exactly what he was thinking. How could she not? After nine years, she knew him so well. He was like another part of her. Like a leg or an arm. And after he was amputated from her life, she'd feel the ghost of his presence for years.

And yet she couldn't stay. She just couldn't. Certainly not now. She'd had her own reasons for leaving before. But now that he was going to marry awful Kitty Biedermann? Well, being in love with your boss was bad enough. But when that boss was married? That would end in nothing but misery.

And her best chance of breaking free of Derek permanently was to stick it out for now and win this damn challenge they had going. Then she'd not only be free of Derek, but she could go back to culinary school— half a continent away. Poughkeepsie, New York had never looked so good.

"Of course I'll stay. After all, we have a lot to accomplish in the next week."

"Oh, for goodness sake." Kitty waved her perfectly manicured hands in a display of dramatic pique. "If you're really not the nanny, then I certainly hope the first thing you plan to accomplish is hiring one."

Derek opened his mouth to answer, but Raina beat him

to the punch. She really wanted to deliver this news herself. "No, not at all. In fact, Derek just let the nanny go." Kitty didn't need to know it was a temporary situation. "He's just determined to learn to do all of this on his own."

"You can't be serious." Kitty's lips curled downward in distaste when Derek didn't deny it.

"Yep," Raina said with a grin, feeling spitefully mischievous. "He's completely enchanted with the idea of being a dad. He's been staying up with Isabella all night long. Feeding her. Changing her dirty diapers. The whole shebang."

At the phrase "dirty diapers" Kitty actually shuddered in revulsion.

Maybe she'd been laying it on a little thick, but— Raina justified to herself—Kitty deserved to know what she was getting into. And so did Derek.

"You know, I almost feel sorry for Kitty," Raina murmured to Isabella as she leaned over to blow a kiss onto Isabella's naked belly before tugging her onesie back into place after a diaper change.

After Isabella's giggles of delight faded, she shot Raina a disbelieving glance.

"I said almost," Raina protested. Still she felt the need to explain. "I'm just saying, when she agreed to marry a billionaire diamond magnate, she probably didn't know she was signing up for a life of burp cloths and diaper genies."

Raina rolled Isabella onto her belly and off of the towel she'd spread out on the office floor to change Isabella's diaper. Isabella wobbled onto her elbows to watch as Raina folded the towel, then set it on the wingback leather chair beside the diaper bag.

From the executive bathroom in Derek's office, she still had a good view of Isabella's spot on the floor, so Raina gave her hands a quick wash in the sink and poured herself a glass of water.

Derek clearly needed a break from dealing with two such difficult women at the same time—the two being Kitty and Isabella, because Raina refused to consider herself one of the difficult women. It had been three days since Kitty had shown up. The heiress had spent so much of that time at the spa, Raina was surprised she had any surface left on her body to buff, polish or exfoliate. When she wasn't at the spa, she'd devoted her time to disrupting the tentative bond forming between Derek and Isabella. The result of which were tears, pouting and temper tantrums. And Isabella wasn't very happy, either.

The average man would have buckled under the strain by now. Derek, clearly no ordinary man, appeared to be getting by solely by clenching his jaw. Frankly, she was amazed he hadn't yet cracked a tooth. Perhaps her last act as his assistant should be rescheduling his biannual dental exam. Just to be sure.

So Raina insisted she drive downtown herself to pick up the custody papers Derek's lawyer had drawn up. She'd absconded with Isabella before Derek could protest. The documents were safely tucked into her briefcase and now she and Isabella were killing time hiding in Derek's office.

By the time Raina had made it back from the bathroom, Isabella had wiggled forward a good four inches.

Raina grinned. "Man, any day now, you're going to be crawling. Then it'll be, look out world!"

Isabella shot Raina a look of defiant arrogance so like her father's, Raina couldn't help chuckle. "Yeah, I know, I'm stating the obvious. Of course you'll be crawling soon. I'd never dream of implying you wouldn't be."

She plopped down on the floor beside Isabella. Studying the infant's flawless skin and bright blue eyes, Raina felt her heart contract.

"Honey, you could not be any cuter. That Kitty's an idiot. Anyone would be thrilled to be your stepmom."

Isabella grinned as if to say she thought so, too. Then she wobbled forward with a jerk. Raina moved to help the girl onto her knees. Isabella mewled in protest as if to insist she could do it herself.

"You are just like your father. A nice healthy dose of that Messina independence."

As soon as the words left her mouth, a pang of loss sliced through her chest, killing her good mood. How in the world was she going to leave him?

To Isabella she said, "The only thing I don't understand is why you don't see it."

Isabella had grown to tolerate Derek's presence, but only just. By the end of his first week of taking care of Isabella, he'd mastered all of the basics: feeding, swaddling, and yes, even car seat installation. Raina almost would have believed her job was done. That she was a shoo-in to win the challenge. Except for two things. First off, Derek was still approaching fatherhood with all of the enthusiasm of an inmate on death row. Secondly, Isabella would hold out her arms and smile eagerly at anyone who walked through the door, except Derek.

"I can only assume you're just as stubborn as he is."

Isabella looked annoyed. As if to prove Raina wrong, she tried to wiggle forward again, only to fall flat on her face.

"Ouch. That had to hurt." Raina snatched Isabella up in her arms and waited for a howl of pain that never came. Isabella merely clenched her toothless jaw and wiggled to show she wanted back down.

"Like I said, stubborn and determined. And apparently, holding a grudge."

"I assume you're talking about Derek?"

Raina jerked her head around to find Kitty standing in the office doorway. As always, she was dressed like the vamp from some forties noir movie. Which only made Raina more aware of the inadequacies of her own, very practical wardrobe. But hey, at least when Isabella spit up on her, it only ruined a fifteen-dollar T-shirt from Target.

With a patently false smile, Kitty slinked into the room, shutting the door behind her. "I hope you don't mind me butting in on your morning. When Derek mentioned you'd come to the office, I decided to take the opportunity for us to talk. Woman to woman."

Raina gritted her teeth and returned Kitty's smile. She had no intention of being won over by Kitty's platitudes, but Kitty didn't need to know that.

"What exactly did you want to talk to about?"

"Why, Derek, of course." Kitty perched on the very edge of one of the leather wingback chairs. "And this foolish notion he has about raising that child himself."

The way she said the words "that child" as if Isabella was a vial of the small pox virus made Raina feel like Kitty was grating her inch-long acrylic nails across Raina's bare nerves. Even Isabella must have noticed the slur, because she reached a hand out to Raina as if seeking reassurance.

Raina held her close. "I'm not sure I agree that it's a foolish notion. Family is very important to Derek." Then, because she couldn't resist, she added, "You of all people surely know that."

A flush crept into Kitty's cheeks. "Of course. But Derek mentioned that his brother—Dexter is it?—is very fond of the child, as well. Wouldn't he and that fiancée of his be better suited to raise the girl?"

Not wanting to tip her hand, Raina carefully kept the outrage from her voice. "Are you suggesting that Derek give custody of Isabella to Dex and Lucy?"

Kitty forced another overly benign smile. "You can see, I only want what's best for her, can't you? If Dexter and Lucy care for the girl, why shouldn't they raise her? After all, she is Isabella's aunt."

"And Derek is her father," Raina said clutching Isabella to her chest. "I've always felt the best environment for children is with their parents."

"Well, normally, of course." Kitty shot Isabella a dismissive glance.

"Derek wants to parent her," Raina said. She believed it, too, but she couldn't deny the question nagging at the back of her mind. Did Derek honestly want Isabella or was he just doing what he thought was right? Always the right thing for the family.

"But Dallas is so much more wholesome than New

York. It's a much better place to raise a child, don't you agree?"

The apparent change in topic rocked Raina back on her heels for a moment. "Well, yes, but—"

"Then you see my point. I knew I could rely on you to be sensible." Kitty stood, clutching her bag under her arm. "You'll talk to Derek for me then?"

"Talk to Derek? I don't understand."

"Explain to him that Isabella should stay in Dallas with Dexter."

"But Derek lives in Dallas, too."

Kitty chuckled as she headed for the door. "Of course he'll always keep a house in Dallas. But he's certainly not going to live here once we're married."

Nine

"Are you sure this is necessary?" Derek didn't quite growl the question, but there was a definite grumble to his voice.

"Huh?" Raina snapped her gaze back toward Derek. Through the haze of her distraction, she'd picked up his tone, but not the gist of his question.

"This." He scowled as he waved a copy of *The Foot Book*. Isabella sat on his lap, her back to his stomach, her feet thumping the leg he'd propped up on his other knee.

The three of them were sitting outside by the pool as a concession to the beautiful day. The sky was a crystalline-blue, the sun bright, the breeze faint, the heat bearable.

Kitty had spent less than three minutes glaring at Raina and Isabella on the back patio before declaring the sun "entirely too bright" and the temperature "ridiculously hot" before storming back inside to—as she'd put it—take a sleeping pill and a nap. Kitty's absence was no doubt a large part of the patio's appeal.

Raina might have felt guilty for driving Kitty off if Kitty weren't obviously pure evil. But since she could put comic book supervillians to shame, Raina wasn't too concerned.

Derek, however, seemed less than thrilled with the arrangements. He held up the book for her to see.

"Ah," she said. "The reading. Yes, it's necessary."

Derek's scowl deepened, but he eased back against the chair, settled Isabella against his chest and began reading again.

The sight of them together tugged mercilessly at her heart. Their faces wore identical expressions of serious concentration. Isabella sat, nestled in the crook of his arm, her tiny hands clutching his forearm. Her lower lip wobbling occasionally as if she might jump in and pick up reading where he left off.

Who was Raina kidding? If she wasn't careful, Derek plus Isabella would send her straight to heartbreak without passing Go or collecting two hundred dollars.

How did Kitty not get this? How could she be in the same room with them for even five minutes and not see how much they needed each other?

Obviously, Isabella needed her father. Because her mother, Jewel, clearly wasn't prepared to step up to the plate, it was all the more important that she have a loving father in her life. Raina knew firsthand that when you'd been abandoned by one parent, you really needed the support and love of your remaining parent.

But Isabella's future happiness wasn't the only thing at stake. If Derek let Isabella go—if he failed at this— he'd never forgive himself. Family was important to him. Raina knew that better than anyone. But perhaps more than that, he needed a child in his life. Someone fun and lighthearted. Someone who could help him reclaim a little bit of his own too-short childhood. Isabella could do that for him.

But only if he let her. So far, he'd approached father-hood with such seriousness. He hadn't yet found any of the wonder or joy in raising a child. And if Kitty had her way, he probably never would.

Before Raina could even consider how to fix things, Derek once again lowered the book.

"She's only five months old. She can't possibly understand what I'm reading to her."

"Maybe," Raina conceded, closing the magazine she'd been pretending to read. Ever since her discussion with Kitty the day before, she'd been trying to broach the subject of Kitty's evil plan to dominate the world—or at least Derek's life—but so far she hadn't found a tactful way of saying, *By the way, your fiancée is the spawn of hell.*

Instead she said, "Research shows that early exposure to literature can dramatically improve a child's language and reading skills."

Derek frowned, but read another page before looking back up. "Did the studies say at what age—"

"Dex did it."

Derek straightened a little in his chair. "Well, if Dex can read Dr. Seuss, then so can I."

"Actually, I think Dex was reading Jane Austen. *Emma,* maybe. Derek, I have a question about—"

"Jane Austen?" Derek sat forward, indignation written clearly on his face. As he spoke, he gestured with the book. Isabella waved a hand in the air, reaching for it. "Dex got to read her Jane Austen and you have me reading her 'Left foot, left foot, left foot, right'?"

"Look at her, she loves it. It doesn't matter what you read. Just that you're reading." Raina sucked in a deep breath, ready to try again. "About Kitty—"

But before she could get her question out, Derek stood, dropped *The Foot Book* on the empty chair and carried Isabella into the house.

Raina hopped up to follow. "It's not a competition."

But Derek ignored her. She caught up with him in the library, hovering in *D*'s between Dickens and Dostoyevsky. Isabella was propped on his hip, her tiny hands clutching his shirt, her head cocked to one side as she studied his face.

Raina's heart fluttered in her chest. For the first time, he looked like a father. He looked at home with Isabella. Confident and relaxed.

Well, okay, as relaxed as he ever looked. He still bristled with barely contained energy. And of course his natural competitiveness had been piqued. He was reaching for *Crime and Punishment,* when she pressed her hand against several leather bound spines to block his progress.

"You can't read her Dostoyevsky."

"You said it didn't matter what I read. That she'd enjoy anything."

"I meant anything you enjoyed reading to her. No one enjoys *Crime and Punishment.* Not college students and certainly not infants."

Derek's spine stiffened defiantly. "I enjoyed it."

"No, you didn't." The big liar. "You haven't read a novel in years. You read *Business Weekly*, *Time* and occasionally those abbreviated versions of popular business books they publish for busy executives." He looked ready to protest, but she didn't give him a chance. "And don't try to read any of those to Isabella, because she won't enjoy them any more than you do."

She ran a finger down the row of *D*'s until she found what she was looking for. "If you insist on reading her one of the classics, try this one." She plopped her favorite Sherlock Holmes novel into his hands. "It's pretty short and I think you'll like it. And will you please just listen for a second?"

"Sure." Derek nodded absently to her as he read the spine of the book then flipped it open to the first page.

"I was just… The thing about Kitty is…" Damn it. How did you tell someone they'd made a colossal mistake? Particularly someone who never made mistakes? Finally, she blurted out, "Derek, you don't like New York, do you?"

He didn't even glance up, his attention apparently already focused on the book. "I don't think I've ever read it."

Suppressing a groan of frustration, she clarified, "The city, not the book. I'd just gotten the impression that you didn't particularly like it there."

"New York's fine," he said distractedly, jostling

Isabella to his other hip. "I like the hotel you usually book me at, if that's what you're worried about."

"The Plaza? Yes, people usually do like it. But you wouldn't want to live in New York, would you?"

This warranted a look up. "Live in New York? City? Why would I live there? Corporate headquarters are here."

She didn't know whether to be relieved or worried by his answer. "You do have an office in New York," she pointed out.

"Just a satellite office. And it's our smallest one." As if she didn't know more details about the office than he did. "What's this all about?"

She hesitated, just shy of spilling the beans about Kitty. But wasn't that something he'd have to figure out for himself? When this week was done, she'd be out of his life. Why continue to be a go-between for him and Kitty? She didn't work for Kitty and she owed her nothing. Sure, Raina wanted to make sure Isabella was protected, but that wasn't her job, either. Not really. She wasn't part of the family. Dex and Lucy would step in if they needed to. If Derek yielded to Kitty's wishes. And frankly, if that happened, Raina would be thankful she wouldn't be here to watch. "Just curious," she mumbled. "I thought maybe you'd been thinking about moving corporate headquarters there."

"I would never do that. New York is too expensive to house headquarters there. It would cost a fortune to move everyone there. It's out of the question."

"That's what I thought." But he'd already taken the book and Isabella and headed out for the patio again, leaving her alone in the library.

She stood in the empty room, staring at the doorway through which Derek had just disappeared, fuming. "Well, crap."

He'd sworn he'd never move to New York. And she recognized all his reasons as perfectly logical. Yet she knew Kitty would not be swayed by mere logic. Yesterday, Kitty had made it clear she had no intention of living in Dallas, let alone raising Isabella as her own.

Since he was seventeen, every decision he'd made had benefited Messina Diamonds. And it wasn't just about success in business or making money, but rather because he saw the company as his family. Why wouldn't he? Until his father had died just over a year ago, the three Messina men had worked side by side to make the company a success.

If he married Kitty, best-case scenario, she'd be an awful mother to Isabella. Worst-case scenario, she'd bully him into giving her up to Dex and Lucy. Though, now that Raina thought about it, at least that way Isabella would be raised by loving parents. But she knew Derek well enough to know he'd never forgive himself if he didn't raise Isabella himself.

The worst part was, Raina knew Derek would be torn. He saw marrying Kitty as the best thing for Messina Diamonds. But he didn't know yet that she planned on moving him away from company headquarters. Yes, they could relocate to New York, but at what cost?

True, Derek probably wouldn't cave to Kitty's pressure, but then she'd just make his life miserable in return.

Why does it matter? part of her asked. *He's a grown-*

up. He can take care of himself. Plus, he's unknowingly stomped all over your heart. Why do you even care if he's miserable?

But she did care. And if she walked away from him now, if she let him make this huge mistake, she'd never be able to forgive herself. She'd cared about him for too long to simply walk away when he needed her most.

"I just can't let you do it."

At her announcement, Derek looked up from the book he'd only just opened. He'd already returned to his chair in the shade by the pool. Isabella, nearing her naptime, had settled back against his chest, her eyelids drooping.

"You can't let me read *The Hound of the Baskervilles* to Isabella?"

He hoped he'd misunderstood, because he was curious to know what kind of book Raina had picked out for him. Besides, she was right. It had been years—decades maybe—since he'd read anything for pleasure.

For a moment, Raina just stared at him, her hands propped on her hips, her brow knitted in confusion. "No. I…I just told you to read that to her."

"I know."

"I mean, I can't let you marry Kitty."

"Is this about the kiss?" He looked down at the book before slowly closing it.

Raina snapped her mouth shut. Her cheeks flushed an alluring shade of pink before she answered. "No. This isn't about that."

He studied her, taking in her pursed lips and the

flash of her eyes. Perhaps inevitably, he was flooded with the memory of what it had been like to kiss her. To tap into that passion and heat she'd hid from him for so long.

"We should probably talk about that."

"No!" But her answer came too quickly. "We shouldn't. It was a mistake. I haven't given it a second thought."

Her lie couldn't have been more obvious if he'd hooked her up to a polygraph machine. Obviously she hadn't had any more luck forgetting their kiss than he had. And he'd certainly tried.

"This isn't about…" Verbally she fumbled. "About that. This is about Kitty and how she's completely wrong for you."

He let her change the subject only because he wasn't sure talking about the kiss would do him any more good than thinking about it had. Wanting one woman while you were engaged to another was damn inconvenient. Having both of them in his home, along with Isabella, had nearly induced an aneurism. Which might actually be less painful to endure.

"You claim you want to have a real relationship with your daughter," Raina continued. "It's important enough to you that you bargained away the last two weeks of my employment so I could teach you how to be a good father." Her voice rose sharply as she spoke, crackling with emotion. "But none of it is going to matter if you marry Kitty, because she's going to be a very bad step-mother."

"She'll learn."

"No, Derek. Unless you're hoping she'll learn to be a different person."

"You've made it pretty clear you don't like Kitty."

"It doesn't matter whether or not I like Kitty. The question you should be asking yourself is if *you* like Kitty. For that matter, when you asked her to marry you, did you even know her?"

But before he could say anything—or even give her question much thought—Raina continued. "Oh, I'm sure this all seemed like a good idea at some point. I'm sure that finding the perfect wife and getting married was all part of your five-year plan."

He cringed. Because marrying Kitty Biedermann actually was part of his ten-year business plan. The perfect bridge between opening the diamond-cutting branch in Antwerp and growing the market for those diamonds.

She must have noticed his response, because her gaze narrowed in annoyance. "Just forget about your plans for a minute, which I know will be hard for you. Trust me, I know how much you love to plan things out. I've spent the past nine years of my life making sure your plans worked out the way you planned them."

"Raina—" he began, surprised by the resentment tingeing her words, but she cut him off.

"Marriage shouldn't be a business decision. You're joining your life with hers."

Somehow, Raina managed to sound vehement rather than bitter. The strength of her conviction made him think. What would it mean to join his life with another's, as Raina so poetically put it?

What would it be like to have that one person he trusted completely? That person he saw every day?

Who challenged him without being antagonistic? Who always had his best interests at heart?

And yet, when he tried to picture that person, Kitty wasn't who came to mind. Raina was.

Because, after all, wasn't that what he had with Raina already?

Ten

"You think I'm silly, don't you? That I'm being overly romantic?"

The idea that Raina might be his perfect wife startled him into answering honestly. "No, I don't."

She blinked in surprise. "Well, at least you're willing to admit it. Because I know you, Derek. I know in your heart you don't just want a business merger. You want a real marriage. Like what your parents had."

"My parents' marriage was far from perfect."

"I'm not saying it was. Just that they were well-suited for each other. Your father had this crazy idea that he'd find diamonds where no one else thought to look for them. And she supported him through everything. Years of living in near-poverty in remote locations. Dragging the family from place to place. She put up with it because she loved him."

Derek thought of his parents and their relationship. His mother hadn't just put up with it, she'd loved it, too. Before his mother had developed cancer, their lives had been one adventure after another. And when the disease finally picked her off, his dad had continued ferociously searching for diamonds, but he'd lost the joy in doing so.

Raina was right. His parents had been perfectly matched. Their life together was anything but conventional, but their love for each other had been the glue that had held the family together.

Could he ever have that kind of relationship with Kitty? He was beginning to have doubts.

"Perhaps we can both agree that my parents' relationship was unusual. I don't expect that from Kitty."

"But maybe you should."

"Kitty is an astute businesswoman. She's smart and she's savvy. She'd never do the kinds of things my mother did. She'd never put her life on hold to follow her husband to Bolivia at the drop of a hat."

"I'm not even talking about Bolivia. I'm talking about just relocating to Dallas."

"But she did come to Dallas when I needed her to." Though that seemed like a small enough concession in the scheme of things. Yes, she'd come to Dallas, but she hadn't shown the least bit of interest in Isabella. She'd never even held the girl in her arms.

Raina sucked in a deep breath and he could see her mustering the courage to say something. Finally she blurted, "She's not going to live here."

He was less surprised by her words than by her absolute certainty. This wasn't a guess.

"She's told you that?"

Nodding, but not meeting his gaze, she said, "Yes. It happened to come up."

And then she fell silent, her hands twisting, her teeth nibbling on her pinkened lips. There seemed to be more she wanted to tell him, but couldn't quite force out.

"Raina…" he prodded.

Her gaze darted to his. "What?"

"Is there more?"

She frowned, her lips pursing in disapproval and her brow knitting. Finally, she said, "You need to talk to her about these things."

These things, she'd said. And as she'd done so, her eyes flickered to where Isabella lay asleep against his chest. Just as quickly, she looked back at him, meeting his gaze defiantly. She wasn't going to tell him any more.

But she didn't need to. He could put the pieces together well enough all on his own. Apparently, Kitty had told Raina not only that she didn't want to live in Dallas, but also something about Isabella. It didn't take a genius to figure out what that might be.

Anger knotted his belly. Damn it.

"I don't suppose I ever considered where we would live. I always assumed Dallas."

"But—" Raina protested.

He cut her off. He didn't need her recriminations, as well as his own. "Breaking off my engagement now would be disastrous. It would ruin our working relationship with Biedermann Jewelers."

She bumped her chin up. "There's more at stake here than your relationship with Biedermann Jewelers. Forget about what's right for Messina Diamonds for a minute and think about what's right for you. You've been so focused on business for so much of your life, you've forgotten how to want things for yourself."

As he watched her, sitting there beside him, with her cheeks flushed from the exertion of her arguments, her eyes sparkling with vehemence and desire pumping through his veins, he could think of only one response. "Trust me. I still know how to want things for myself."

She sucked in a breath and his eyes dropped involuntarily to her mouth. That luscious, perfect mouth of hers. If they'd been alone, he would have kissed her. If he'd been free, he would have done much more.

Frustrated with himself, as well as the situation, he couldn't help but point out the obvious. "What about you, Raina?" he asked. "Do you still know how to want things? You talk a good game, but when was the last time you did something for you?"

She blinked, surprise rocking her back in her chair. She took a moment to answer. "We're not talking about me."

"Maybe we should be." He shifted the sleeping Isabella in his arms. "What is it you want?"

She seemed to sway toward him. This time it was her gaze that dropped to his lips. His mind flashed back to the moment in the driveway when her lips had first pressed against his. How her entire body seemed to melt into his.

He knew without a doubt that she wanted him. Probably as much as he wanted her. As desire stretched between them—as hot and as inescapable as the noonday sun—everything else faded away, until all that remained was his need for her.

"What is it you desire?" he pressed, wanting to hear her say it aloud, even if she'd never act on it.

But instead of the admission he expected, she blurted out, "Kitty doesn't want to raise Isabella. She wants you to give custody of her to Dex and Lucy."

Raina paused. No doubt waiting for him to gasp in shock. But frankly, he wasn't surprised. Anything that took that much gumption to say had to be particularly bad. Still, even though he expected it, her words sent a pang of longing through his chest. His arm automatically tightened around Isabella where she lay curled against his chest.

He glanced down to see her sleeping there. At some point in the past few minutes, she'd fallen asleep against his chest and he hadn't even noticed.

When he didn't respond, Raina blinked rapidly, then continued. "Here's the thing, Derek. Isabella is your daughter. And if you want to raise her, then you should get to do that. Regardless of whether or not it's best for the company. Regardless of whether or not it was part of your ten-year plan."

Raina swung her legs over the side of the lawn chair and planted her feet firmly on the ground, leaned toward him as if every molecule in her body was willing him to listen to her.

"But if you don't want her, if you can't love her with all your heart, if the thought of giving her up doesn't make every cell in your body recoil, then maybe you should step aside. Dex and Lucy adore her. If you can't love her like they can, then maybe it would best for Isabella to let them raise her."

Even as she said the words, his body tensed, flooding with parental adrenaline. He wouldn't let anyone take Isabella away from him.

But before he could say that to Raina, she'd disappeared back into the house. Moments later, he heard her car start up in the front drive.

He let her go, too frustrated with himself to go after her.

He'd predicted Kitty would have a problem with Isabella, but he'd assumed that he'd be able to win her over. However, now that Kitty was in Texas, he was seeing her in a whole new light. Who was he kidding? Kitty hadn't been hiding who she was, he just hadn't seen her.

Obviously, she didn't have a maternal bone in her body. It wasn't something they'd ever discussed before. But it would be a problem regardless of whether or not Isabella was in the picture. He wanted children. He wanted Isabella to have a mother who would love her as if she were her own.

Kitty would apparently not be that mother. But as he'd pointed out to Raina, how could he end things now?

After all these years of careful planning, all his goals for Messina Diamond's future were unraveling. All because of one little baby.

Raina had accused him of forgetting how to want things for himself. Maybe there was some truth to that. But it had never bothered him until now. His entire adult life, every decision he'd made had been based on what

was best for the company. It came first in his life.
Always.

It had to. Because Messina Diamonds wasn't just a
company, it was a family company. It was his father's
legacy. Its success was a reflection of all the sacrifices
his parents had made.

And now, for the first time ever, what was right for
the company was not what was right for his family. For
the first time, he was going to have to choose between
them.

Knowing Kitty was evil and doing something about
it were two totally different things. However, Raina
was determined to do something. And she had less
than a week to do it in.

By Wednesday of next week, she'd be free from
this craziness. One way or another, she'd be out of
Derek's life forever. Even if Derek wasn't satisfied
about how he'd bonded with Isabella, even if she didn't
win their bet and the healthy compensation package,
she had to leave Messina Diamonds.

But for now, Raina looked at the soufflé she'd just
pulled out of the oven and wanted to cry. And not just
because the damn thing had fallen in the oven and now
resembled a badly curdled quiche.

Once, a decade ago, she'd known how to do these
kinds of things. She'd lived and breathed soufflés, bro-
chettes and béchamel sauces. She'd been flying through
her first year of culinary school, convinced nothing
would prevent her from being Dallas's hottest new chef.

Now, her familiarity with Hamburger Helper far
outweighed her experience with hollandaise. And

worse still, at the moment, she hardly cared. She never knew a broken heart would hurt more than a shattered dream.

She'd always assumed that leaving culinary school to take that awful job at Messina Diamonds would be the hardest thing she'd ever done. She'd never dreamed that walking away from that same job would hurt just as badly.

"Frankly, I don't see what you're so worried about." Lavender, who'd been working at the kitchen table all evening, poured herself another cup of coffee then reached for the sugar. "So what if he marries the wicked witch of the Upper West Side."

"She's going to ruin his life," Raina protested.

"So what? Hasn't he practically ruined your life for the past nine years?"

"Yes, of course," she muttered dismissively. This was the problem with having a secret crush on your boss. No one, not even your sister, understood when you defended the man who'd found a way to muck up nearly every day off. "It wasn't so bad."

But her protest sounded weak, even to herself. The truth was, the long hours and demanding schedule were most difficult because of her crush. She knew and accepted that this was her own damn fault. If she hadn't been so emotionally involved, she could have drawn better boundaries between her personal life and her professional one.

"I say," Lavender pointed the sugar spoon in Raina's direction. "Let the bastard make his mistakes and stew in whatever misery they stir up." Lavender narrowed her gaze at Raina as if waiting for her to say something.

Finally she gave a resigned sigh. "But you're not going to do that, are you? No, you've just got to be the one to step in a save everyone."

Raina returned her sister's glare. "What's that supposed to mean?"

"You can't ever just let people muddle through things on their own, now, can you? You've always got to be the one who comes to the rescue. Like with Momma. When she had her stroke, what did you do? You dropped out of culinary school and rushed home to help out."

"You're sounding awfully critical for someone who benefited from me rushing home to help out."

Lavender stirred her coffee with a last few emphatic strokes. "Hey, don't get me wrong, I appreciate it. But it wasn't your problem."

"I just did what needed to be done."

"No. You didn't. You, my dear, went above and beyond the call of sisterly duty. You put your whole life on hold. Not just until Momma could get back on her feet, but indefinitely. And now that Momma and the kids don't need you anymore, now that you can finally get on with your own life, look what you're doing. You're inventing this problem that Derek needs you to solve."

"You think I'm *inventing* this problem? Are you saying I'm delusional?" She didn't bother to keep the annoyance from her voice.

"No, I'm just saying you like solving problems for people. You like being needed."

"That is not true!" she protested.

"Then prove it. At the end of this week, when you're finished with this silly bargain you've made with

Derek, walk away. Quit, whether you win or not. Just leave."

"But—"

"And don't let yourself get sucked into this nonsense with his fiancée." Lavender gave Raina a pointed look. "I mean, unless there's some deeply personal reason you don't want him to marry Kitty."

Raina feigned ignorance. "I don't know what you're talking about."

Lavender snatched a dinner roll out of the basket on the table and threw it at Raina's head.

"What?"

"Honestly, Raina. Are you never going to fess up and admit you're in love with Derek?"

Her gaze darted to her sister's. "You knew?"

Lavender rolled her eyes. "Of course I knew. What'd you think, I was an idiot?"

"I… I… Does any one else know?"

"I'm guessing Momma has figured it out. After all, she's always defending him."

"Oh." And here Raina had thought her mom had just figured out where the money came from for the renovations on their house. "The kids?"

"Who, Cassidy and Kendrick? No, they're too involved in their own lives. And Jasmine's been away at school for too long."

"Why didn't you say anything before now?" Raina asked.

"Because, silly, I was waiting for you to say something. You're my sister and my best friend." A glimmer of pain shone through Lavender's words. "I can't believe you never told me."

"I never told you because you hate Derek."

"I don't hate Derek. I've been baiting you, trying to get you to defend him and admit that you're in love with him. You've just been too stubborn to rise to the bait." Lavender cocked her head to the side and studied Raina.

"Why is it so hard for you to admit that the real reason you don't want him to marry Kitty is because you want him for yourself?"

"This isn't about what I want."

"Maybe it should be. If you really love him, then don't just hand him over to Kitty. Fight for him."

Raina sighed as the truth sank in. "Don't you see? Kitty isn't really the problem. Long before she showed up, I was right there in front of him." Pain pierced her heart as she said aloud for the first time what she'd always known, but dreaded admitting. "He just never wanted me."

Raina looked away because she couldn't stand to see the pity in her sister's eyes.

After a moment, Lavender said, in an overly bloodthirsty voice, "If that's the case, then why do you care? Why not just let him muddle through on his own?"

Good question. "Because I love him" was the only answer she could give. "Even though he doesn't love me, I can't let him make a mistake that I know he'll regret for the rest of his life. Not if I can do something to stop it."

Raina knew Derek desired her, there was no doubt about it. He didn't love her, didn't want a real relationship with her, but he did desire her. And she'd never seen even a fraction of that kind of spark in his dealings with Kitty. So what it came down to was this: he was too honorable a man to sleep with one woman while remaining engaged to another. Which meant the easiest, fastest way to convince him to dump Kitty was to seduce him herself.

But did she really want to be that woman? Geesh, did *anyone* want to be that woman? And perhaps, more to the point, did she really have it in herself to seduce him? After all, she'd spent the past nine years disguising herself as the consummate professional. Personality-less, humorless, sexless.

Could she cast all of that aside to seduce a man like Derek? He may not be the connoisseur of women Dex was before meeting Lucy, but he was certainly no slouch.

Compare that to her experience with men, which was—to say the least—limited. She'd had one brief passionate affair with Trey, whom she'd met in culinary school and who had dumped her when she'd dropped out. Since then the men she'd dated simply hadn't inspired the kind of excitement she wanted in a relationship. Not that she'd had time for a relationship anyway.

And who was she kidding? No man had lived up to her ideal. No man could compete with Derek.

If she was honest with herself, if she left Messina Diamonds without at least trying to seduce Derek, she'd never forgive herself. And she might not ever get over him.

Did she really want to be the other woman? No. But it was the only way everyone could get what they wanted. She would to save Derek from the mistake of marrying Kitty. Isabella would get the devoted father she needed without the evil stepmother. And she would get the closure she so desperately needed. Even Kitty would get what she wanted—a life in New York City without a pesky stepdaughter to slow her down.

It was a win-win situation. If only she could pull it off.

Eleven

"We need to talk."

At first, Kitty, who was lounging by the pool, didn't give any sign she'd even heard him. After a long moment, he cleared his throat.

Finally, she raised a languid hand to her sunglasses and nudged them onto her head as she wedged herself up on her elbow. She sighed, managing to sound beleaguered. As if he was imposing upon her rigorous schedule of luxuriating by the pool in the mornings and getting massages in the afternoon.

"Where's the child?" she asked.

"Isabella is with her aunt." Since Kitty seemed determined to avoid Isabella's company, he'd finally broken down and called Lucy to take Isabella for the morning so he could discuss things with Kitty. If Raina was right and Kitty didn't want to raise Isabella, he'd rather know now than later.

"Thank goodness." Kitty swung her legs over the side of the lawn chair and stood.

"You seem relieved." As if that wasn't a profound understatement.

"Well." She smiled a very catlike smile as she closed the distance between them. "Having a baby around does make certain things very awkward."

She stopped mere inches away from him. The delicate bikini she wore showed off her curves to their best advantage. Her body, buffed and oiled from all her time at the spa, gleamed with the falsely golden tone of a sprayed-on tan. She was as beautiful as she was unappealing.

She moved to plaster her body against him, but he deftly sidestepped her.

"And you don't want children of your own someday?"

Kitty waved a dismissive hand. "I'm sure I will. But I'm only twenty-nine. I'm not ready for that yet."

Only twenty-nine? Raina was only twenty-eight. And yet she seemed so much more mature. So much more what he wanted.

And yet, Kitty's words were believable. At twenty-nine she obviously wasn't adult enough to share her life with a child. She wasn't ready to give up being the center of attention.

If Derek was going to marry, then he definitely wanted someone who was ready. Not just ready to be a wife, but a mother also. He'd had the responsibilities of an adult from the time he was a teenager. The last thing he needed was to have to wait for his wife to grow up, too.

"This isn't going to work," he stated baldly.

Kitty's expression soured. "I knew it would come to that." She crossed her arms over her chest. "You would really dump me for a child?"

"She's my child."

Kitty's nose bumped up in the air, obviously offended. "And for her, you'd blow a business deal that would make you millions? I suppose you think that's noble or something."

"No. I merely think it's necessary."

Kitty's expression grew even more unpleasant. "You'll regret this," she sneered. "You'll never do business with Biedermann Jewelry again."

She would have stormed back into the house in a fit of pique, but he stopped her with a hand on her arm. She stopped and turned back to face him, her eyebrows raised in obvious indignation.

He took her left hand in his, raising it so her three-carat engagement ring sparkled in the sun. "That's where you're wrong, Kitty. Biedermann Jewelry will do business with us, for one reason. You like diamonds. The prettier the better. And right now, the best diamonds in the world are coming out of our mines. So I'm guessing you'll eventually get over being dumped by me. Especially if I let you keep the ring."

For a moment, Kitty continued to glower at him. Then she snatched her hand away and her scowl began to fade. "We'll see."

* * *

Unless he was mistaken, Raina was trying to seduce him.

Sure, there was a chance that seduction wasn't at all what she had in mind and that his exhaustion was leading him astray. After a week and a half of late-night feedings and stress-filled days, that was certainly a possibility. But it was a slim one. Or maybe it was just that he'd spent most of the week and a half with Raina. Not the businessy, professional Raina he was used to, either, but the tempting, sexy Raina who seemed determined to wear down his self-control. So maybe he was just being overly optimistic.

He'd known Raina a long time and he'd never before seen her like this. Playful. Enticing. Absolutely, charmingly seductive.

At the moment, she stood just a few feet away from him, in the kitchen. In the past few days, the shorts she'd been wearing had gotten shorter and shorter. Her tops, skimpier and skimpier. The shirt she wore today was a clingy cotton of sea-green, with a V-neck deep enough to reveal the tops of her breasts. Her shorts revealed the entire length of her slender tanned legs.

Once again, Isabella was with Lucy and Dex. It wasn't an arrangement Derek wanted, but Dex had insisted. Apparently he'd been offended that Lucy got to watch Isabella without him a few days ago. So when he had some time free in his schedule, he'd absconded with his niece.

Derek had agreed only because he'd been wanting time alone with Raina to talk. However the instant Dex left with Isabella, Raina had launched into an elaborate demonstration of how to make homemade baby food.

He looked up from the banana Raina had him mashing. "Are you sure this is necessary?"

"Of course," she chirped, bending over to pull a pan of sweet potatoes out of the oven.

If she hadn't been so bound and determined to cook her way through the afternoon, he would have pulled Raina into his arms and kissed her senseless. But first they needed to talk. And she wasn't letting him get a word in edgewise. As it was, his frustration with her was proportionate to his sexual frustration.

"In the next few weeks Isabella is going to start eating solid foods. And there's no reason she can't have a tempting variety of foods, rather than just bland cereal and jarred mush." Raina swiped her finger through a bowl of something orange. "Here, try this."

She held her finger up to his lips. Heat sizzled between them when his gaze met hers. Slowly he lowered his mouth to the dollop of food she'd extended to him. When he sucked her finger into his mouth, her eyelids fluttered closed for a second.

The food was warm and sweet on his tongue. "Delicious," he murmured. "What was that?"

"Butternut squash." Her eyes snapped open and pink flushed her cheeks.

"Positively tempting."

"I told you it would be better than that jarred stuff. Now, don't you agree it was worth it?"

He glanced around the kitchen. It looked almost as if a hurricane had hit. Dishes of food lined the counters.

The sink was piled high with the dirty food processor bowls and blades. Ice cube trays were stacked ready to go into the freezer, each full of tiny individual servings of different foods.

"I don't know that I'm ready to admit to that."

She chuckled. "What are you complaining about? Your housekeeper will be here tomorrow to clean up the mess. And in the meantime, you've made enough food to feed Isabella for several weeks."

He studied Raina, wondering if she really was trying to seduce him. She'd been wiggling around the kitchen all morning. Bumping innocently against him. Offering him tasty nibbles of various foods. Her eyes were flashing. Her cheeks were flushed. She was beyond tempting. And he was once again seeing a different side of her.

"You love this, don't you?"

She looked up at him, cocking her head to one side. "What?"

"This." He gestured to the kitchen. "Cooking."

"I do." She shrugged, turning her back to him to spoon the butternut squash into yet another ice cube tray. "I always have loved it."

"I didn't know."

"There are—"

"I know." He cut her off, turning her to face him again. "There are a lot of things I don't know about you." He brushed a golden lock of hair off her forehead and tucked it behind her ear. "Was I such a tyrant to work for that you felt like you could never be yourself around me?"

Her brow furrowed. "No," she began, but then abruptly

broke off. Her frown deepened as she seemed to be considering what to say next. But then she smiled seductively and wiggled a little closer. "As a matter of fact—"

But he stepped out of her reach before she touched him. All morning long it had been like that. Every time he tried to talk to her, she deftly sidestepped the conversation by throwing temptation in his face. Frankly he was getting tired of it.

"Raina, stop it."

Her frown turned into a pout. Not one of Kitty's aren't-I-cute pouts, either, but a genuinely annoyed scowl. She quickly buried it beneath another seductive shimmy.

"Derek," she murmured, her voice low and honeyed.

She was tempting, all right. But she wasn't what he really wanted. He wanted the real Raina. Not the coolly professional Raina who'd been his assistant. Not this overly sensual seductress. He wanted the woman who could give as good as she got. Who would get in his face and bully him if she needed to.

So when she reached out her fingers to brush against his cheek, he grabbed her hand in his and held it. "Raina, we need to talk."

Anger flashed through Raina like a spring flood. She'd been trying her damnedest to seduce Derek all morning. And the bastard just wouldn't crack. Well, she'd had enough. She snatched her hand from his and waggled her finger at him like a scolding mother.

"You know, a lot of men would be more than happy with me."

He blinked in dispassionate surprise. "Excuse me?"

"I'll have you know that some men consider me quite a catch." *Men she hadn't dated because she'd been too in love with Derek.*

"I'm sure they do."

His baffled tone didn't diminish her pique at all. "Men at work ask me out all the time. Mike Kaplan from payroll. Scott Thompson from research. Geesh, even Dex used to ask me out on occasion." She stopped mere inches from him. "I'm pretty." She poked him in the chest.

Surprised, he retreated until he bumped against the counter. "You are," he agreed in a tone so amiable it only angered her more.

"I'm smart." Again she poked him in the chest.

"Undoubtedly."

"I keep in shape."

"I'm sure you do."

"And I've been told that I have a very nice rack." She punctuated each of the last three words with an additional poke.

His gaze automatically dropped to her chest. But she didn't give him a chance to admire the view he'd been ignoring for far too long. Instead, she prodded his chin up with her poking finger and forced him to meet her gaze.

"So why in the world—" she propped her hands on her hips, her anger and indignation so tight in her chest she thought she might pop "—have you been fighting this so hard? Are you really that devoted to Miss-I-Don't-Care-About-Anyone-But-Myself Kitty or are you just that dang stupid?"

As the last of her tirade shuddered out of her, she

looked—*really* looked—at his face. At the expression of shock that had settled over those perfect patrician features of his. As she did so, the words that had poured unrestrained from her lips echoed in her mind and flooded her with embarrassment.

She dropped her arms to her side. "Or maybe I got this all wrong and you really don't want me at all."

His shocked lingered on his face for only a second before being swept off. And then Derek, who never chuckled, never grinned, never so much as cracked a smile—laughed out loud.

The sound so surprised her, she withdrew from it, immediately backing up a step, stumbling over her own feet.

Yet she didn't fall. Derek caught her. Snatched her up in his arms and pulled her to him. With one arm at her back and the other behind her head, he dragged her mouth to his and kissed her. Her feet dangled above the floor as he plastered her body to his.

His mouth was hot and powerful over hers. His lips were relentless in forcing a response from her. After a moment, her surprise gave way to elation and she opened her mouth, granting him access, welcoming him into her.

Her legs, still dangling uselessly, automatically snaked around his waist and her arms around his shoulders, her hands plowing into his hair.

His kiss was powerful. Unyielding. Everything she'd ever dreamed of. And somehow so much more. Yet not enough. Not nearly enough.

How long had she dreamed of this moment? How long had she waited, wondering how he would taste again? What it felt like to touch him once more? To have him touch her?

The muscles of his shoulders bunched powerfully beneath her hands. So strong. So wide. So capable of carrying burdens.

His hair, which her fingers had itched to touch so many times, was just as silky as she'd imagined. Plush and full, slightly springy. She imagined spending hours just stroking it. If there weren't other parts of his body she wanted to stroke more.

For an instant, panic flashed through her, lapping over her desire. What if he stopped? What if he came to his senses? What if this was her one chance? Her only opportunity to touch him? To taste his kiss? To feel his hands on her body?

As transitory as passion was, his could fade at any second. Melancholy mingled with passion as tears prickled at the backs of her eyes. She clasped her hands on either side of his face, trapping his lips against hers in case he decided to pull away.

Only then did she realize he was already moving. Not away from her as she'd feared, but up the stairs. Cradling her body against his, with her legs wrapped around his waist as she clung to him, he was carrying her toward the one room in his house she'd never been in. His bedroom.

Relief surged through her and on its heels a new burst of passion. But not just desire, something else, as well. Joy perhaps, because at last he was hers. Only for this moment. Only for this brief flash of delight. But he was hers.

He made short work of the hall at the top of the

stairs, striding past the guest bedrooms and Isabella's room to the double doors at the end of the hall. Once through them, he kicked them closed behind him. She had only the briefest impression of masculine, dark-stained furniture and pristine cream fabrics before he lowered her to his silken-covered bed. He followed her down, resting his weight beside her, propping himself up on one elbow.

She pulled away from his kiss, retreating just enough to see his face. The face she knew so well, better than her own, better than that of beloved members of her family. Before now, she'd thought she'd seen every emotion he was capable of. Cunning, determination, anger, satisfaction.

But she'd never seen this. This heavy-lidded desire was completely foreign to her. A shiver coursed through her as need washed over her, ratcheting up the heat pumping through her body.

"You're sure this is what you want." His voice came out a low rumble, replete with barely restrained passion. As he spoke, his hand burrowed under her shirt, claiming the skin of her body just as he'd claimed her mouth already.

"This is what I've always wanted," she answered honestly.

He pulled back to study her face. "Surely not always?"

She rolled her eyes in exaggerated exasperation. "Yes. Always."

"Then I was a fool not to see it before."

"Yes, you were," she agreed.

Her answer was swallowed by his kiss. Her body

gave way to his demands, her breasts surging up to fill his hands, her legs parting to accept his weight. Her hips bucked again him.

All of which only reminded her that they both wore far too many clothes. Her hands sought the wash-worn linen of his shirt, tugging at the buttons, desperate to undo them. To reveal the skin beneath. The chest she'd ached to touch so many times.

Raina's touch threatened to make him lose all control. He felt as though he'd been waiting forever for this moment. For this chance to peel her clothes from her body. To touch her silken skin and feel her tremble beneath him.

His hands shook as he pulled her T-shirt over her head and cast it aside. Her breasts were encased in a plain, cream-colored bra. Like Raina herself, the garment was simple and unassuming. There was nothing fancy or pretentious about it.

Somehow the simple packaging only enhanced the breasts it contained. He didn't need luxurious lingerie to desire Raina. She was temptation enough all on her own.

He didn't need tricks or gimmicks. Raina naked, her bare skin next to his. The heat of her body. The sensation of her heart thundering in her chest when he pressed his palm to her breast. The quick intakes of her breath. The soft sigh of her release. The moisture between her legs wicking through her panties. The physical evidence of her desire.

All that was enough to send him over the edge. She was enough.

She was all he wanted. All he needed. And he'd

indeed been a fool not to see it before now. But he was done being foolish. Now that she was his, he would never let her go.

As their clothes fell away, he rolled off of her for the briefest moment, only to return to her, sheathed in a condom, completely ready for her. But he didn't enter her yet, though her body surged up to meet his, her breasts full and aching, her nipples hard and puckered. Her stomach trembled beneath his palm as anticipation shivered down her spine into the deepest heart of her.

Every cell in her body vibrated with the need to press itself against him. To be absorbed by him. The feel of his naked skin against hers helped stem her agitation, but also made it worse.

As his hands moved over her body, desire blossomed within her and she felt herself unfold before him, pulsing and moist, clinging to him, desperate for his touch. For the release only he could give.

Stroke after stroke, his hands pushed her closer and closer to the edge. She clutched at him, pulling him farther on top of her, desperate for all of him. And then he surged into her, dominating her completely.

Pleasure washed over her body in wave after wave, undulating under her skin until she thought she might explode, until she did explode, leaving her fulfilled and satisfied in every way.

In every way except one. For along with the tortured moans of need, there were words trapped on her lips, held there by the last remnants of her common sense. Words that—despite the passion of the moment—some part of her was smart enough to hold inside. *I want you. I need you. I love you.*

They were words he'd never hear. Because this act of love wouldn't bind them together. In the end, it would drive them apart.

Twelve

Lying in bed, in Derek's arms, her body replete and heavy from their lovemaking, Raina should have been as content as she'd ever been in her life. She'd certainly never felt more sexually satisfied.

Despite that, she was acutely aware of how limited her time would be with him. She had, at best, a few short hours before she'd have to rise from his bed, dress and leave him. Possibly forever.

Part of her wanted to simply relish the physical intimacy they shared, however a greater part of her yearned for a more emotional connection. How could she help but be curious about him? She had so many years of questions and this would be her only chance to have them answered.

So she propped herself up on her elbow and asked

the first question that popped into her head. "Why did you hire me?"

His eyes blinked open, his expression sleepy and sated. "Because I needed an assistant."

"Well, yes, I get that." Absently she ran her hand over the contours of his chest. "But let's face it, I was young and inexperienced. Surely you could have found someone better."

He slanted her a look tinged with humor. "What do you mean? The woman I hired was twenty-four and had spent the previous five years working as an assistant for J. P. Morgan."

She stared blankly at him for a minute. "J. P. Morgan? Was that really the name I put on my résumé?"

He nodded. "That's right. According to your résumé, you were the assistant to the famous nineteenth century industrialist."

She laughed, dropping her face to his chest to hide her embarrassment. "Okay, I knew I was lying on my résumé, but I thought I was just making up a name. It must have been stuck in my head from high school history or something." She looked up, her laughter fading. "So why did you hire me? Obviously you knew I'd lied about my experience on my résumé."

"Not just about your experience," he pointed out. "About your age, too. You were only…what was it? Eighteen?"

"Nineteen. But just barely." She propped her chin on his chest. "At first, I thought I was just lucky. That you didn't check the references I'd made up or that you hadn't noticed that the age listed on my résumé was different than the info I filled out for personnel. But I know better than that now. You never would have hired me without checking that stuff. You just chose to ignore it. Why?"

"Pure ruthlessness. Obviously you were desperate for the job. I was desperate for someone who would work really hard. I knew if you were willing to lie for the job, working long hours wouldn't be a problem. So I took a chance. It worked out for both of us."

She chuckled. "And here you always pretend to be so conservative. That was a pretty big risk for Mr. Gotta-Plan-Everything-Out. Looks like maybe you have a reckless streak I didn't know about."

"Maybe I'm better at taking risks than you think."

She sucked in a deep breath. Time to stop beating around the bush. "You want to do something really reckless? Get rid of Kitty."

It was probably stupid of her to bring up Kitty at a time like this, knowing that the very topic of conversation would drive a wedge between them. But how could she not try, one last time, to convince him she was right. Regardless of what happened next, their relationship would end in a matter of hours anyway. This was the end of the line for her. Soon she wouldn't be his assistant or his lover. She'd have no right to tell him her opinions. Now was all she had.

He said nothing, his expression blank, his emotions carefully controlled.

But this time, he didn't argue with her about it. She sucked in a preparatory breath. Okay then. Once more into the breach, so to speak.

"You obviously don't love her, or you wouldn't have slept with me." This may be her last chance to convince him, so her words came out of her in a rush. "As far as I can tell, you don't even find her very attractive. If you do, you do a good job hiding it."

Derek opened his mouth as if to speak. But she held up her hand and plowed ahead. "And I know you said you admire her as a businesswoman, but frankly, in the time she's been here, I haven't seen her work that much. She's spent way more time at that day spa than she has doing business. And to be honest, I'm not even sure she likes you very much, either, because she's spent more time there than she has with you."

She had to pause to breath, but she ended up holding her breath, waiting for Derek's backlash against her comments.

But instead of the brusque annoyance she expected—which she'd received the last time she'd criticized Kitty—he merely smiled.

The smile was thin and closemouthed, but there was definitely humor there. "Kitty hasn't been at the day spa all this time. I sent her home three days ago."

"Sent her home? I don't understand." But anxiety pinched her stomach. Had Kitty returned to New York to plan the wedding? Was it possible Raina had misread Derek all along and he had no intention of letting a little sex with his assistant get in the way of his marriage?

"You're not still going to marry her, are you?" Disgust crept along her nerve endings as she said the words.

"Would that bother you?"

She recoiled back against the headboard. "Are you joking?"

"I am," he said wryly. "Apparently I'm not very good at it." But before she could feel anything other than the faintest pang of relief, he added, "I sent Kitty home because I realized you were right. I can't possibly marry her."

"Oh."

"You were right all along. She'd be a horrible step-mother."

"Wait a second. You sent her home three days ago?"

"Yes."

"*Three* days ago?" Annoyance propelled her back onto her knees so she could face him on more even terms. "So all morning, I've been throwing myself at you trying to break up an engagement that had already ended?"

"She took it better than I thought she would. Frankly, she was probably relieved. However, she did keep the ring."

Ignoring his comment, she asked incredulously, "If you knew you weren't going to marry her, then why didn't you tell me?"

"To begin with, I tried to talk to you about it this morning."

"You didn't try very hard."

"I assumed you'd figured it out."

She could only stare at him, baffled. "You *assumed* I'd figured it out? How could I possibly have guessed you'd ended your engagement?"

"For starters, Kitty wasn't here. Besides, you were obviously trying to seduce me."

Humiliation burned her cheeks. Had her attempts been so clumsy? "Right. Obviously."

He tugged at her hand, so she fell against his chest. Gently he brushed a lock of hair from her forehead. "You were charming."

His touch was tempting, but his tone that of someone placating a pouting child. She pulled away. "I'm glad I could amuse you."

Well, wasn't that just perfect. She was pouring out her heart and he found her charming.

She scrambled to the edge of the bed, tugging at the sheet to bring it with her. The fact that he was sitting on the corner, making her efforts largely fruitless, only frustrated her all the more. "I was throwing myself at you at every opportunity."

"I know. It was cute." He followed her to the edge of the bed, swinging his legs over the side while brushing her hair off her shoulder to expose the curve of her neck.

Again, that amused expression crossed his face, really truly pissing her off. "Cute? Do you know how hard that was for me? How I wrestled with my conscience?"

"Wrestled with your conscience?"

"Well, of course. You're an engaged man. At least, that's what I thought."

He stilled in the process of leaning close to nibble at her neck. "After nine years, you don't know me well enough to know I'd never sleep with you if I was engaged to another woman?" His expression was pained, his tone accusatory.

"That was kind of the point." Maybe she should have felt a pang of sympathy for him, but her own emotions were running too high for that. "I knew if I could get you to sleep with me," she explained, "then you'd break up with Kitty. It was the only way I could think of guaranteed to make you dump her."

His expression went stoically blank. "You're saying you slept with me solely to end my engagement?"

This time, she couldn't ignore his reaction. "I did it for Isabella," she protested. "I did it to save her from Kitty."

His expression darkened as he pulled away from her. "I didn't realize sleeping with me was such a sacrifice."

She rolled her eyes, giving the sheet a final tug to pull it free. "Don't you dare get offended. Don't you dare pretend I've wounded your considerable pride."

"The woman I planned to marry just told me she slept with me only for the welfare of my child. How am I supposed to feel?"

His words pulled her up sharply. "The woman you plan to marry?" she repeated numbly.

He stared at her for a moment before his lips curved into one of those rare smiles she'd fallen so hard for. "Of course, silly. Of course I plan to marry you. What did you think *this* was about?" He gestured to the two of them.

Shock knocked her back. Clutching the sheet to her chest she considered his words. Funny, but marriage was the one place she'd never considered that "this" might lead.

"I…" She studied his face, looking for clues to what he expected from her. She found none. "I don't know what to say."

"Say yes."

God, she wanted to. And maybe she even would have. If only it hadn't been for Isabella.

But he'd broken up with Kitty because she wouldn't be a good mother. If Raina did say yes, she'd never know if he'd asked only because she *would* be a good mother.

When he sensed her hesitation, he kept talking, angling to seal the deal. And dang it, he really should have kept quiet.

"Come on, Raina. This is what you want. It's what you've always wanted. You said so yourself."

Once again he took her hands in his. This time she felt too numb to pull them away.

"You're not going to throw this all away," he continued. "You know how good we are together."

"How good 'we' are?" She snatched her hands away as frustration beat at her. "The only 'we' I know about is the 'we' that shows up at the office every day. As in, 'we make a great team, Raina,' and 'we really nailed those negotiations.' Is that the 'we' you mean?"

Confusion flickered across his face. "What are you saying? That if we get married you don't want to work at Messina Diamonds anymore?"

Her hands spasmed on the sheet. Part of her wanted to throw something at him. Unfortunately, all she had handy were clothes and bed linens. She wanted something heavy. And possibly pointed.

"For the last two weeks I've been saying I don't want to work at Messina Diamonds."

He shrugged. "Fine. You won't work there."

Dragging the sheet behind her, she crossed to where her clothes had fallen and snatched them up. Before she could put them back on, she spun back to face Derek.

"You just don't get it, do you?"

"Get what?" he asked, but really, his blank expression was answer enough.

"I'm your assistant, Derek." While she spoke she tugged on her clothes with fast, jerky movements. "It's what I've always been. That's all there's ever been between us."

As she fumbled with the snap on her shorts, he rose and went to her. He pulled her to him, kissing her roughly. For a moment, she let herself enjoy the sensation of his lips pressed to hers, knowing it was the last time she'd ever feel it.

He pulled back, searching her face. "How can you say that when we just slept together?"

"Well," she said as she stepped away from him, distancing herself from his touch and from her greatest temptation. "That's a mistake I won't make again."

Because there were things she wanted more than a husband. She wanted a husband's love.

By the time Raina made it to her car, every muscle in her body was trembling. Anger and humiliation churned in her stomach, as sour and unpleasant as food gone bad. How had she been so wrong? How had she made so many mistakes?

She'd thought so long and hard before developing her plan to seduce Derek. She'd been sure it was the only solution. That in the end, her actions were justified, even though sleeping with an engaged man went against everything she believed in. And for what? Only to find out that he wasn't engaged at all. That her sacrifice meant nothing. Worse still, he'd asked her to marry him, simultaneously fulfilling all her dreams and destroying them, because he'd asked for all the wrong reasons. Anger roiled through her. Derek had done this. But she was also to blame.

This would teach her to think twice before putting someone else's needs above her own morals.

From here on out, she was doing what was best for her and her alone. And that started with going back to school. With shaking hands, she reached into her purse and pulled out the flyer from the Culinary Institute of America that Lavender had given her just the other day. Lavender was right. It was time—past time—she started doing things for herself.

Thirteen

"So, let me get this straight," Dex said, the laughter barely suppressed in his voice. "You asked her to marry you?"

"Yes." Derek nodded grimly, sorry he'd brought it up. Annoyed, he turned his back on his brother to stare out over the back patio and pool. It was dark enough in the twilit yard that he could see Dex's reflection in the glass. Dex sat, sprawled in one of the living-room chairs, casually confident. Derek should have known better than to bring this up to Dex.

"And she said no?" Dex asked.

"Correct."

"It serves you right," Dex managed through his laughter.

"This isn't helpful," Derek said through clenched teeth.

Just then, Lucy waltzed into the living room, Isabella gurgling happily on one hip, a recently warmed bottle of formula in one hand. She handed the bottle to Dex, then playfully swatted the back of his head.

"Behave," she ordered. "And Derek's right. This isn't helpful. Besides, it's not as if I said yes to you the first time you asked."

Derek turned around, eyebrows raised in speculation.

Dex straightened in his chair. "That's why this is so amusing. Besides, that was different."

Lucy scoffed. "How was that different?"

Dex pulled Lucy—and Isabella, too—down onto his knee. "You were always going to marry me."

"I was—"

"You just didn't know it yet when you said no."

He nuzzled her neck and for a moment, she let him, before she levered herself off his lap. Handing Isabella over to him for feeding, she smoothed her shirt, obviously fighting the blush that had crept into her cheeks.

"Don't listen to Dex. He doesn't know what he's talking about. It was sheer luck and generosity on my part that I ever said yes." She leveled a look at Derek. "Why don't you tell him exactly what she did."

Derek frowned as he recalled how badly the conversation had gone. One minute she'd been warm and willing and in his arms, the next she'd been storming out of his house and possibly his life.

He tried to trace through the conversation to the point where it all had gone wrong. "She said she didn't want to work for Messina Diamonds anymore."

Lucy circled her hand in a "keep it coming" gesture. "And you said…"

"I said she didn't have to work there if she didn't want to."

Lucy winced. "And then?"

"And then she got mad and stormed out," Derek admitted. Dex chuckled, drawing the full force of Derek's frustration. "You think this is funny?"

Dex shrugged. "Of course it's funny."

Lucy slanted him a look. "Hey, Mr. Pick-A-Diamond-Any-Diamond, you didn't do any better the first time out of the gate."

"See? That's why this is so funny," Dex explained.

Derek ignored Dex's pathetic excuse for a sense of humor and turned to Lucy. "So how do I fix this?"

The irony of the situation wasn't lost on him. For the past nine years, it was Raina who'd been fixing problems for him. Now that he needed her most, she wasn't here to help him.

"Well," Lucy began. "You asked her to marry you, but never told her you loved her. The problem isn't where she works. It's how you see her. She wants a husband who loves her. Not a boss."

Lucy's words seemed to reach into his chest and tug at his heart. Until this instant, Derek hadn't let himself think about his feelings for Raina.

Did he love her?

She was the glue that held his world together. Not because she'd assisted him in reaching every goal he'd set for himself, but because her faith in him gave him the strength to constantly push himself.

He needed her in his life. She was the one person

he simply couldn't function without. It wasn't because of what she did for Messina Diamonds. He couldn't care less about that. No, he'd want to marry her even if she never set foot in Messina Diamonds again in her life.

She was all he needed.

Of course he loved her. He was a fool not to have seen it before now. But then, he'd been foolish about many things lately. Not just about Raina.

"So I just need to tell her how I feel."

Again Lucy winced. "I'm afraid it's too late for that. You're way past just telling her you love her. You're going to have to prove it."

Derek glanced over at his daughter, who sat cuddled against her uncle's chest, blissfully drinking her bottle. He waited for the stab of jealousy. For the feeling of incompetence he'd first felt when watching Dex's ease with Isabella. It didn't come.

Finally what Raina had been trying to tell him sank in. What did it matter if Dex gave her a nickname? What did it matter if Izzie loved her aunt and uncle? Wasn't it far better for her to be an open and loving person, who shared that affection with many people in her life?

Of course he wanted her to love him, too. But that would come with time and hard work, just like everything else in his life that had been worth having. He hadn't built Messina Diamonds into the billion-dollar business it was in two weeks. So why had he expected to build a relationship with his daughter in that time?

And yet, the thought of doing that alone, without Raina—not her help, but just her, by his side—pulled at his insecurities and threatened to close off his throat.

Watching Dex and Lucy with Izzie, he wondered if he was making the right choice. They'd be good parents to her. Who was he kidding? They'd be great parents. And he couldn't shake the feeling that maybe she would be better off with them. Or more to the point, that she might always love them more.

Yet, even as pain welled in his heart at the thought, he knew he wasn't about to relinquish custody to them. Izzie was his. She was a part of him in a way nothing else was. Not even Messina Diamonds.

Maybe it didn't matter whether or not she loved him. Maybe the only important thing was that he loved her. And he did. Far too much to ever let her go.

Izzie loved with a child's openness and innocence. The love of an adult was more profound and all consuming. Loving Izzie made Derek vulnerable in a way nothing else ever had. Except loving Raina.

She may make him crazy, but he did love her.

Being here with Dex and Lucy, watching them together, only reinforced what he already knew. He needed Raina. No one else challenged him and made him think the way she did. No one else completed him. There was no one else with whom he wanted to share his life.

And just as he was now prepared to work hard to build a relationship with Isabella, he was more than ready to do whatever it took to get Raina back. To convince her they belonged together.

Izzie may have made him a father, but it was Raina who would make them a family.

The Dallas-Fort Worth International Airport was as busy as always, but she was used to traveling for business, which allowed her certain perks. Like being dropped off by the limo service and access to the airline's platinum lounge.

For today's flight, Cassidy had dropped her off at the airport on her way to classes. Raina had said a tearful goodbye to the rest of her family before leaving her house. It would be months before she saw them again. This was undoubtedly the longest she'd be away from them since she'd left for culinary school the first time.

As Raina settled into the faux leather swing chair in the waiting area at the gate, she couldn't help comparing that day to this one. She'd been so young—only eighteen—eager to take the culinary world by storm, thrilled at having been accepted to the prestigious Culinary Institute of America.

Today, she just felt tired, the emotional toll of the past two weeks having worn down the excitement she should feel about finally heading off to pursue her dream.

After a few minutes of bored people-watching, she settled back into her chair for the forty-five-minute wait for her flight into JFK airport, her coffee in one hand, the latest issue of *Food and Wine Magazine* in the other.

Not long had passed before the sound of giggling baby filtered through the background noise of the airport bustle. The delightful trill—so full of joy— made her heart ache. Raina kept her head doggedly down, her attention firmly on the magazine.

All baby giggles sounded alike. It wasn't Isabella. There was no point in looking up, hoping to catch one last glimpse of the little girl who'd captured Raina's heart just as surely as Derek had.

"I told you we'd find her."

Raina's head jerked up involuntarily at the sound of Derek's voice. He stood beside her, Isabella strapped into a stroller, giggling as she tried to wiggle free.

Derek lowered himself to the chair beside Raina, nudging her bag aside with his foot so he could wheel Isabella closer to him. "She doesn't like this stroller. She keeps trying to escape."

Raina just stared blankly at him, struggling past her stunned silence. "What are you doing here? And how did you get past airport security?" Then she held up a hand to ward off his explanation. "Never mind. I don't want to know. If you bribed someone to let you through or committed some security violation just so you could show up at the airport and harass me, I don't want to hear about it."

"What makes you think I came to harass you?"

His expression looked pained, but she didn't fall for it. "Because I know you. You don't give up. No matter what. And you just can't stand letting go of a perfectly good employee."

"Technically, you're still my employee."

She gaped at him. "Oh. Even better. You're in complete denial."

"No. I'm not. You gave me a letter of resignation, but your contract says you're supposed to deliver a duplicate copy to personnel, which you never did. I never fired you. So you're still an employee." He leaned over to unbuckle Isabella's straps and lifted her from the stroller. "I'd fire you myself, but according to the deal you negotiated, then I'd have to give you five hundred shares of Messina Diamonds stock."

"I don't want the damn stock."

"That's good, because my contract says that combined, me and members of my immediate family can't own more than forty-five percent of the company."

"What does that have to—" And then comprehension dawned. She laughed cynically. "Derek, only you could propose and talk about business in the same sentence. If this is how you proposed to Kitty, no wonder it took her four years to accept."

"And only you would insult and say yes in the same sentence."

She felt her blood pressure spiking with annoyance. Damn arrogant man.

"I'm not saying yes."

His expression turned suddenly serious. "I'm not letting you go, Raina."

Something inside of her weakened under the intensity of his expression. In that moment, he looked so much like the man she'd fallen in love with: single-minded, determined, unwavering. How could she defend her heart against the very qualities she'd fallen in love with?

And yet, those were all the reasons they couldn't be together. It was that same strength and determination that kept him married to his work.

She leaned forward, needing to make him understand, because she could only do this once. "This isn't how I want to live my life. I don't want to be your assistant forever."

"Is that what you think? That I asked you to marry

me because I wanted to keep you as my assistant? Because I don't want an assistant. I want a wife."

"Do you even know the difference?"

"I've already promoted your friend Trinity to be my new assistant. She was thrilled."

"I'm not talking about my job at Messina Diamonds. I'm talking about the fact that Messina Diamonds will always come first for you. Which means regardless of whether or not I work there, sooner or later, you'll end up treating me like your assistant again. Because you'll never love me as much as you love that company."

"I left Kitty for you. Is that what you want me to admit?"

"Kitty was never the reason we couldn't be together. She was just an excuse. Just a distraction. The real reason we can't be together is because I'll always come in second with you."

"Isabella—"

"I'm not talking about Isabella." At the sound of her name, Isabella, who until now had been bouncing playfully on his lap while he spoke, propelled herself toward Raina, forcing her to catch the child in her arms. Something in Raina's heart contracted at the sweet weight of the girl in her arms. "I'd never ask you to put my needs before hers. She's your daughter. I just want to be with a man who puts me before his work. I deserve that."

He leaned back in his chair, twisting to stare out at the busy terminal. "So that's it then? You're just going to leave for culinary school and never look back?"

"How did you know about—"

"It wasn't hard to find out."

"I don't know if I'm supposed to be flattered or annoyed that you had someone digging around in my business."

"I guess what you want is some guy who'd be willing to put his whole life on hold and follow you to New York."

She scoffed automatically, but as the thought settled in, she nodded. "I guess that is what I want. I think I deserve to have someone make sacrifices for me for a change."

"Then we're both in luck." He reached into the front pocket of his jacket and pulled out a sheaf of airline tickets.

"Tickets to New York?" She eyed the tickets with no less suspicion than she would one of those trick packs of gum. No way would she fall for this and get her fingers snapped.

"A one-way ticket to New York."

She cast him a sideways glance, caution weighing down her hope. "You can't move to New York."

"Why not?"

"Because you're you. You live and breathe work. You're not going to put all that on hold while I go to culinary school."

He shrugged, his mouth twisting into a smile that was almost sheepish. "Of course not. We'll live in Poughkeepsie, which is just a thirty-minute helicopter ride to Manhattan. Dex can run the Dallas office. You're the one who said he wanted more responsibility."

"But you don't want to live in New York. You wouldn't move there for Kitty. You said so yourself."

"I don't love Kitty. I love you. I was too stupid to realize it before. But you've made me a better man."

"Derek, I don't—"

"You can't tell me you don't love me. I won't believe you. You're too nice of a person to have bullied and tormented me otherwise."

She cringed playfully. "I certainly did give you a hard time, didn't I?"

"I probably deserved it."

"Probably?" she asked.

"Definitely." He traced a finger down her cheek. "So what do you say? I love you. Will you marry me?"

Tears sprang to her eyes. To hide them, she buried her face against Isabella's tiny neck. "I don't know what to say."

"Say yes. We're boarding in about ten minutes. I bribed the airline clerk to get me a seat next to yours. If you tell me no again, it's going to be a really long flight."

She looked at him from over Isabella's head. "Yes," she said simply.

For all these years, she'd dreamed he'd say such wonderful things to her. She just never dreamed it would really happen.

Epilogue

"Is it normal to be this nervous?"

Raina pressed a shaking hand to her stomach, then instantly jerked it away, hoping her sweaty palm hadn't stained the beaded silk of her wedding dress.

Lucy, who stood beside her with Isabella in her arms, merely shrugged. "I wasn't. But then, Dex and I had such a small ceremony." She gave Raina a sympathetic smile. "You're the one who wanted all the fuss of an enormous society wedding."

"True." She peeked around the edge of the heavy wooden door at the back of the church where her sisters were already parading down the aisle toward the pulpit. The sight of Derek standing beside the minister calmed her nerves. Somewhat. "I just want everything to be perfect."

"Pefec!" chirped Isabella, who at seventeen months was just beginning to talk.

Kendrick, dressed in a tux and looking so very mature, chuckled.

Lucy beamed with pride. "That's right, sweetie. Perfect." She smiled at Raina over Isabella's head. "You'll do fine." Then she set Isabella down and clasped her hand. "It's showtime for you."

Isabella, dressed in yards of fluffy white chiffon, tugged her hand away. "Me do!"

She grabbed the basket of rose petals from Lucy and clutched it desperately to her chest. Then she trotted off through the doors just as fast as her tiny legs would carry her.

This was not how it had gone during the numerous rehearsals. With a shrug of resignation, Lucy followed her.

Kendrick held out his arm to Raina. "Your turn, princess."

As she made her way down the aisle, the last of her nerves vanished. Nothing she'd ever done had felt more right. Derek had spent most of their year-long engagement convincing her just how much he loved her. He'd banished any doubts she had that Messina Diamonds might come before the people in his life.

No groom could be more eager. No bride more loved.

When Raina was midway down the aisle, Lucy finally caught up to Isabella at the front of the church. Isabella still held tightly to the basket of petals, only a few of which had made it to the ground. Instead of going to stand beside Dex, who held out his arms to her as they'd practiced in the rehearsal, Isabella stopped before Derek, dropped the basket, dumping the petals in a pile, and held up her arms to him.

"Up, Daddy!"

Dex threw back his head and laughed.

Derek flushed red, but couldn't hide his pleasure. With a loving smile, he bent to pick up his daughter as she launched herself into his arms.

As he met Raina's gaze over the top of Isabella's head, Raina's heart felt ready to burst. It may have taken them a long time to get here, but they were truly a family.

* * * * *

Don't miss Emily's next book,
WEDDED INTO THE BILLIONAIRE'S DYNASTY
part of The Hudsons of Beverly Hills,
available February 2009 from Silhouette Desire.

Here's a sneak peek at
THE CEO'S CHRISTMAS PROPOSITION,
the first in USA TODAY *bestselling author*
Merline Lovelace's HOLIDAYS ABROAD *trilogy*
coming in November 2008.

American Devon McShay is about to get the Christmas surprise of a lifetime when she meets her new client, sexy billionaire Caleb Logan, for the very first time.

Silhouette®

Desire

Available November 2008

Her breath whistled out in a sigh of relief when he exited Customs. Devon recognized him right away from the newspaper and magazine articles her friend and partner Sabrina had looked up during her frantic prep work.

Caleb John Logan, Jr. Thirty-one. Six-two. With jet-black hair, laser-blue eyes and a linebacker's shoulders under his charcoal-gray cashmere overcoat. His jaw-dropping good looks didn't score him any points with Devon. She'd learned the hard way not to trust handsome heartbreakers like Cal Logan.

But he was a client. An important one. And she was willing to give someone who'd served a hitch in the marines before earning a B.S. from the University of Oregon, an MBA from Stanford and his first million at the ripe old age of twenty-six the benefit of the doubt.

Right up until he spotted the hot-pink pashmina, that is.

Devon knew the flash of color was more visible than the sign she held up with his name on it. So she wasn't surprised when Logan picked her out of the crowd and cut in her direction. She'd just plastered on her best businesswoman smile when he whipped an arm around her waist. The next moment she was sprawled against his cashmere-covered chest.

"Hello, brown eyes."

Swooping down, he covered her mouth with his.

Sheer astonishment kept Devon rooted to the spot for a few seconds while her mind whirled chaotically. Her first thought was that her client had downed a few too many drinks during the long flight. Her second, that he'd mistaken the kind of escort and consulting services her company provided. Her third shoved everything else out of her head.

The man could kiss!

His mouth moved over hers with a skill that ignited sparks at a half dozen flash points throughout her body. Devon hadn't experienced that kind of spontaneous combustion in a while. A *long* while.

The sparks were still popping when she pushed off his chest, only now they fueled a flush of anger.

"Do you always greet women you don't know with a lip-lock, Mr. Logan?"

A smile crinkled the skin at the corners of his eyes. "As a matter of fact, I don't. That was from Don."

"Huh?"

"He said he owed you one from New Year's Eve two years ago and made me promise to deliver it."

She stared up at him in total incomprehension. Logan hooked a brow and attempted to prompt a non-existent memory.

"He abandoned you at the Waldorf. Five minutes before midnight. To deliver twins."

"I don't have a clue who or what you're…"

Understanding burst like a water balloon.

"Wait a sec. Are you talking about Sabrina's old boyfriend? Your buddy, who's now an ob-gyn doc?"

It was Logan's turn to look startled. He recovered faster than Devon had, though. His smile widened into a rueful grin.

"I take it you're not Sabrina Russo."

"No, Mr. Logan, I am *not*."

* * * * *

Be sure to look for
THE CEO'S CHRISTMAS PROPOSITION
by Merline Lovelace.
Available in November 2008
wherever books are sold,
including most bookstores, supermarkets,
drugstores and discount stores.

REQUEST YOUR FREE BOOKS!

2 FREE NOVELS PLUS 2 FREE GIFTS!

Passionate, Powerful, Provocative!

YES! Please send me 2 FREE Silhouette Desire® novels and my 2 FREE gifts (gifts are worth about $10). After receiving them, if I don't wish to receive any more books, I can return the shipping statement marked "cancel". If I don't cancel, I will receive 6 brand-new novels every month and be billed just $4.05 per book in the U.S. or $4.74 per book in Canada, plus 25¢ shipping and handling per book and applicable taxes, if any*. That's a savings of almost 15% off the cover price! I understand that accepting the 2 free books and gifts places me under no obligation to buy anything. I can always return a shipment and cancel at any time. Even if I never buy another book, the two free books and gifts are mine to keep forever.

225 SDN ERVX 326 SDN ERVM

Name	(PLEASE PRINT)	
Address		Apt. #
City	State/Prov.	Zip/Postal Code

Signature (if under 18, a parent or guardian must sign)

Mail to the **Silhouette Reader Service:**
IN U.S.A.: P.O. Box 1867, Buffalo, NY 14240-1867
IN CANADA: P.O. Box 609, Fort Erie, Ontario L2A 5X3

Not valid to current subscribers of Silhouette Desire books.

Want to try two free books from another line?
Call 1-800-873-8635 or visit www.morefreebooks.com.

* Terms and prices subject to change without notice. N.Y. residents add applicable sales tax. Canadian residents will be charged applicable provincial taxes and GST. Offer not valid in Quebec. This offer is limited to one order per household. All orders subject to approval. Credit or debit balances in a customer's account(s) may be offset by any other outstanding balance owed by or to the customer. Please allow 4 to 6 weeks for delivery. Offer available while quantities last.

Your Privacy: Silhouette Books is committed to protecting your privacy. Our Privacy Policy is available online at www.eHarlequin.com or upon request from the Reader Service. From time to time we make our lists of customers available to reputable third parties who may have a product or service of interest to you. If you would prefer we not share your name and address, please check here. ☐

SDES08R

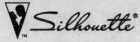
Silhouette®

Romantic
SUSPENSE

*Sparked by Danger,
Fueled by Passion.*

Lindsay McKenna
Susan Grant

Mission: Christmas

Celebrate the holidays with a pair
of military heroines and their daring men
in two romantic, adventurous stories
from these bestselling authors.

Featuring:

"The Christmas Wild Bunch"
by *USA TODAY* bestselling author
Lindsay McKenna
and

"Snowbound with a Prince"
by *New York Times* bestselling author
Susan Grant

Available November wherever books are sold.

COMING NEXT MONTH

#1903 PREGNANT ON THE UPPER EAST SIDE?—
Emilie Rose
Park Avenue Scandals
This powerful Manhattan attorney uses a business proposal to
seduce his beautiful party planner into bed. After their one night
of passion, could she be carrying his baby?

#1904 THE MAGNATE'S TAKEOVER—Mary McBride
Gifts from a Billionaire
When they first met, he didn't tell her he was the enemy. But
as they grow ever closer, he risks revealing his true identity and
motives, and destroying everything.

#1905 THE CEO'S CHRISTMAS PROPOSITION—
Merline Lovelace
Holidays Abroad
Stranded in Austria together at Christmas, it only takes one kiss
for him to decide he wants more than just a business relationship.
And this CEO always gets what he wants....

#1906 DO NOT DISTURB UNTIL CHRISTMAS—
Charlene Sands
Suite Secrets
Reunited with his ex-love, he plans to leave her first this
time—until he discovers she's pregnant! Will their marriage of
convenience bring him a change of heart?

#1907 SPANIARD'S SEDUCTION—Tessa Radley
The Saxon Brides
A mysterious stranger shows up with a secret and a heart set on
revenge. Then he meets the one woman whose love could change
all his plans.

#1908 BABY BEQUEST—Robyn Grady
Billionaires and Babies
He proposed a temporary marriage to help her get custody of her
orphaned niece, but their passion was all too permanent.

SDCNMBPA1008